I0728320

# AMENDING PLANS

*CM Corett*

A NineStar Press Publication

Published by NineStar Press
P.O. Box 91792,
Albuquerque, New Mexico, 87199 USA.
www.ninestarpress.com

# Amending Plans

Copyright © 2018 by CM Corett
Cover Art by Natasha Snow Copyright © 2018

This is a work of fiction. Names, characters, places, and incidents are either the product of the author's imagination or are used fictitiously. Any resemblance to actual persons living or dead, business establishments, events, or locales is entirely coincidental.

All rights reserved. No part of this publication may be reproduced in any material form, whether by printing, photocopying, scanning or otherwise without the written permission of the publisher. To request permission and all other inquiries, contact NineStar Press at the physical or web addresses above or at Contact@ninestarpress.com.

Printed in the USA
First Edition
April, 2018

Print ISBN: 978-1-948608-63-3

Also available in eBook, ISBN: 978-1-948608-54-1

Warning: This book contains sexually explicit content, which may only be suitable for mature readers.

Luc Weston is employed by his uncle as a cartographer. He's an office dwelling creator of maps and plans, but as his uncle's heir, he must learn all aspects of the company. Specifically, surveying. The upside—spending time with the gorgeous surveyor, Rick Masters, in a cozy cabin. The downside—the cabin is in the woods. Luc hates nature, and nature hates him. He's got the injuries and bites to prove it. How can he impress Rick in such a foreign and hostile environment?

Rick Masters can't believe he has to babysit the boss's privileged nephew for two weeks. Come on, the man turned up for a mountain survey wearing skinny jeans and toting a suitcase on wheels. But Luc's attitude and self-deprecating humor has surprised him. Perhaps he's misjudged him? He's nothing like the robust outdoorsmen Rick is usually attracted to, and yet...those skinny jeans sure hug him in all the right places. But Rick has a plan for his life, and a man like Luc Weston could never be part of it. No way!

# Chapter One

LUC WESTON PRESSED his heel down onto the floor to halt his nervous leg jiggling and leaned forward in his chair. "I know what surveyors do! Why do I need to follow one around for two weeks?"

Luc's uncle, Jeremiah Weston, sighed. "I expect all my employees to participate in the job-swap program, and that includes you, Luc."

Needing an outlet for his agitation, Luc stood up and paced around his uncle's office. The workspace was uncluttered, organized, and neat, just like his uncle, and provided plenty of room for pacing. The large tilted drafting board beside the window caught his attention, and he stopped to stare at the displayed survey plan. "I know, I know, but I'm not just an employee. Surely I'm different?" He winced. Okay, that had come out wrong. He hadn't meant to imply he considered himself better or more important than his colleagues, just...different. *Shit.*

Jeremiah frowned. "Yes, you are different. It's important for every employee to understand the various roles within the company, but it's vital for you, Luc. If you want to take over this company one day, you need to experience every aspect of the business. I need to make sure I'm leaving the company with someone who understands not only our drafting practices, but the surveying and other offsite processes too."

Luc drew in a deep breath. When his uncle spoke in his official "boss talk," there wasn't much room for negotiation, but Luc had to try. "Sure, I get that, but I understand the surveying side of the business. I practically grew up here. I've been surrounded by cartographers and surveyors since I was six years old. Hell, old Harry Miller taught me to mark up a surveyor's field book as soon as I could hold a drafting pen."

"Yes, you've gained a lot of knowledge over the years, but hearing stories and anecdotes from a bunch of surveyors is not the same as experiencing what they perform in the field. And yes," he held up his hand as Luc opened his mouth, "you interpret field books as well as anyone, but physically finding coordinates and hammering in marker pegs is another aspect altogether."

"Yeah, I know." He grimaced. "Out in the wilds of nature and all that."

"Is that what's worrying you?"

"Come on, Uncle J. You know how useless I am in the great outdoors. Surely our one and only camping trip convinced you I was destined to be a city boy." Luc's mouth twisted into a wry smile at the memory. He had been twelve years old and had begged his uncle to take him camping in the nearby national park. During the anticipation stage, his excitement had been off the charts. Once they'd arrived—not so much. Between his tent-erecting ineptitude and his determination to trip over every rock, tree root, and tent peg, the experience had soon lost its promise.

And then there were the sounds—scary, predators-coming-to-get-you-in-the-night sounds.

Jeremiah gave him a stern stare. "You're not twelve years old anymore, and this is your career. And the future of our family company. So, you'll do as I ask."

Luc stood, hands on hips, in front of his uncle's desk. "Or what?"

Jeremiah rubbed his hand across his face. "Or nothing. You're twenty-six years old, Luc. You're a damn fine cartographic draftsman—one of our best. I'm not about to ground you like some disobedient teenager, and I'm surely not going to fire you or even demote you, but I will be severely disappointed in you if you refuse to do this."

*Oh, God.* Luc dropped his hands to his sides, and his shoulders slumped. In the past, he had clashed with his uncle over a few issues, and the resulting anger and the consequences were understandable, but disappointment? *Hell, no.* He hated disappointing the man who'd raised him and had always been there for him. No way could he win the argument, but perhaps the details were negotiable. "Okay. Okay, I'll go."

"Thank you."

"But does the surveyor have to be Rick Masters? Can't I tag along with someone else?"

"Why not Rick? Rick Masters is our best and most experienced surveyor, and we were lucky to hire him two years ago. He had job offers from multiple companies. Yes, he can be a little gruff, and he's a man of few words, but I've always found him to be decent and hardworking. I have a lot of respect for the man. What do you have against him?"

"I have nothing against him, but I feel... It's just..." His heart hammered in his chest. How could he explain his feelings for Rick Masters? He couldn't admit—to his uncle—that Rick Masters made his heart race and his dick behave inappropriately every time he caught a glimpse of the man. No, not the type of explanation his uncle would want to hear. He cleared his throat. "Actually, I think I'd get more out of the experience if I paired up with someone else. What about Jessica Taylor or Stan Myers?"

Jeremiah frowned. "If this was coming from anyone else, I'd think they had a problem working with a gay man, but as Rick and you are both gay, I really don't— Ahh!" He nodded. "Are you worried about the gossip, or is there something else you want to tell me?"

"Well, I..."

"You know what?" Jeremiah raised both palms. "I don't want to hear it. What you think or feel about another of my employees is none of my business. You're a professional, and I know you won't let those emotions interfere with your job. The same goes for your dislike of nature."

"Yes, sir." What else could he say? He had no legitimate reason to refuse, and he would have to suck it up and follow Rick around for a while. Two weeks. With Rick Masters.

And field trips into the wilderness.

*Shit.*

# Chapter Two

RICK MASTERS PARKED his truck outside the front entrance of the tall apartment complex. Located in an expensive area of the city, the modern glass-and-concrete building lacked any kind of architectural detail. No doubt, the apartment interiors were also generic and characterless. Rick grimaced. Not his style at all. His focus turned to the blond-haired man waiting for him on the sidewalk.

*Damn it.* Babysitting the boss's nephew for two weeks would be a nightmare. Actually, having someone accompany him on the job for even *one day* would be taxing. He was not exactly a sociable person, but the fact that it was Luc Weston made him want to throw something. Preferably, the prissy little suitcase sitting on the pavement beside Luc. Come on, it had wheels for God's sake. Did the man think they were spending the next two nights in a five-star hotel? He would probably throw a hissy fit when they arrived at the cabin. Rick considered the cabin comfortable and cozy, but the boss's nephew would no doubt think it primitive.

The guy's clothes were just as unsuitable. Skinny jeans and... He glanced down at Luc's newer-than-new shoes and gave a short, sharp laugh. Typical. The boss's nephew obviously had more money than sense because those brand-name hiking boots were crap. One hundred percent about looking good and zero percent performance. His gaze roved over Luc from toe to head, registering a slim yet toned physique, short blond hair, and an annoyingly handsome face—damn it.

No. Totally not his type.

Rick focused on Luc's clothes again. The words "trendy" and "casual" came to mind. Well, he assumed they were trendy; he didn't know a thing about fashion. A T-shirt was a T-shirt no matter how much the cost. And black skinny jeans were snug. They hugged and delineated...stuff, in a way that shouldn't be allowed. With a hard swallow, he dragged his focus from the tempting sight. Previously, he had only seen Luc in the office environment wearing business shirts and ties: a much more professional look. Although, he had to admit, a certain red tie had given him more than a few inappropriate, unprofessional thoughts. His cock twitched.

*No. Don't go there.*

With a harder-than-necessary shove, he slammed the truck door and strode to Luc's side. "Morning." With an abrupt nod, he grabbed the useless suitcase.

"Good morning. I'm Luc Weston."

"I know."

"Okay." Luc's brows pulled down. "And you're Rick, Rick Masters."

"Yes." Right, probably a good idea to use words with more than one syllable and at least try to act semi-civilized. After wiping his sweaty palm on his jeans, he held his hand out to Luc. "Yes, I am. Hi."

Luc smiled and shook his hand. "Hi. It's nice to finally meet you. I-I've seen you around a few times, but we've never been properly introduced."

"No. We haven't." *Damn.* The man had a smooth voice. And a nice smile. He cleared his throat. "Now that's sorted, did you bring food?"

Luc's smile dimmed. "Yes, I brought a cooler. Your email said to bring enough food for an evening meal and two lunches. So…” With a quick hand flick, he indicated the black bag to his left on the pavement.

Rick grunted. The small bag didn't resemble a cooler, more like a man bag. Probably some fancy, expensive thing designed to match the man's outfit. “Never seen one like that before.”

Luc bit his lip, his perfect white teeth worrying the plump bottom lip as his gaze ran over Rick. “No, I guess…someone like you wouldn't have. I mean…”

Rick narrowed his eyes and stared. *Someone like me? Yeah, and fuck you too, buddy.* He spun on his heel and strode to the truck. *Snobbish little prick. I'll give him 'someone like me' and then some.* The rear door of the truck opened with a metallic groan, and he threw the blue suitcase onto the back seat. “Get in.”

Without waiting or caring if Luc followed his order, he hauled himself up into the driver's seat and started the truck. Okay, he did wait until Luc had jumped into the passenger seat as if his skinny jeans were on fire, but he would be damned if he'd ask about Luc's comfort or try to make conversation.

So, his original impression held—Luc was a rich, handsome, entitled asshole.

It was going to be a long two weeks.

# Chapter Three

TREES FLASHED PAST the passenger window as the sturdy truck powered up the mountain road.

*Transporting me into hell.*

Luc Weston clenched his teeth. His first field trip. *Shit.* The outdoors may as well be alien terrain. He was a cartographer—a mapmaking office dweller with a drawer full of ties and one pair of extra-clean running shoes in the rear of the closet. Since his disastrous childhood camping trip, a few half-hearted attempts at communing with nature had all ended in disaster, transforming him from a semi-competent man into a bumbling fool.

The scene outside passed by in a blur of green, topped by a ribbon of brilliant blue. Such a deceptively peaceful mountain setting—just like the silent atmosphere in the truck. Luc arched his tense back and snuck a glance at the driver. *Damn.* Rick still had a stony-faced expression. Another reason this trip resembled a nightmare.

Rick Masters. Surveyor. The ultimate outdoorsman. With windswept, wavy brown hair, golden-tanned skin, a sexy close-cropped beard, and biceps the size of tree trunks, Rick embodied the lumberjack fantasy man. Luc had dreamed and drooled over him from afar for two very long years. Unfortunately, their first real interaction was not turning out to be the stuff of dreams.

"So, Rick, how long have you worked for the company?" Of course, he knew the answer. *Two years, three months, and about a week or two.*

Rick's fingers tightened around the steering wheel. "Two years."

"Oh, that long?" He cringed at his own words. *Worst small talk ever.*

Rick huffed. "Yes. That long. Although, I'm sure, being from the office and all, you wouldn't have had cause to notice 'someone like me.'"

Luc's shoulders slumped. *Oh, God. I deserved that.* As they had stood outside his apartment building, his nerves had kicked in and turned his brain to mush. The prospect of spending two days and nights with Rick had seriously impeded his coherency. As the comment "someone like you" had spilled from his lips, he knew it sounded discriminatory, but the clumsy word flow had been unstoppable.

*But I didn't mean it like that at all!*

His "someone like you" meant rugged and capable—not to mention gorgeous and hot as hell. Someone like Rick would have a regular no-nonsense cooler, not some ridiculous little bag incapable of barely keeping the food cool, let alone frozen.

*Shit.*

With a sigh, he stared at the passing scenery. Trees, rocks, dirt, critters that bite. Honestly, he didn't understand the appeal. The next two days were going to suck.

Not usually one to shirk his work responsibilities, the combination of his aversion to nature and his attraction to Rick had made him desperate enough to try changing his uncle's mind. Not his proudest moment. Despite the fear of succumbing to nerves and appearing an incompetent fool in front of Rick, he had eventually conceded defeat, packed a suitcase, and bought a pair of hiking boots.

The truck shuddered as it shifted gears before slowing and turning down a narrow side road.

He sat up straighter. "Is this it?"

Rick grunted. "The cabin is just up here."

Luc clung to the door handle as the truck dipped and bounced along the rough dirt track with enough force to rattle bones. And then the log cabin came into view, rustic and quaint, nestled among imposing pine trees. It was perfect. As the truck stopped, he looked at Rick. The tense jaw did not bode well. If only they were here under different circumstances.

*Or at least without that stupid comment hanging between us like an insurmountable barrier.*

After stumbling from the truck, he followed Rick into the cabin.

The interior of the cabin did not disappoint. A blue sofa sat facing a stone fireplace, imbuing a rustic, cozy atmosphere. Behind the sofa lay a kitchen, complete with a small wooden table and two chairs. Perfect for a lover's weekend getaway.

He cleared his throat. "It's nice and cozy."

Rick threw the car keys on the table. "It's not the Ritz, but you'll have to make do."

*Shit.* Did Rick intend to continue with the attitude for the next two days? "Look, I wasn't being rude about the cabin. I actually think it's great. It seems to have everything we need, and it has a nice, cozy feel."

Rick stared at him for a moment before giving a nod. "Okay. Sorry." His gesture indicated one of the closed doors. "This is the room I always use, but you can check out both rooms and choose which one you like best."

"No, no, thanks for the offer, but I'm sure the other room will be fine." After shoving his hands in his pockets, he shifted from one foot to the other. Should he say something else? Try to clear the air?

Rick scraped his fingers through his hair, sending the wavy locks into further disarray. "Okay. Let's get settled in. We'll start work in the morning, but for now, I'll chop some wood and light the fire. Can you bring our bags in from the truck?"

"Okay, sure, sounds like a plan." He flashed a smile at Rick before heading outside to the vehicle.

Luc opened the truck's rear door and stared at his small blue suitcase beside Rick's army-green duffel bag—a fitting representation of their differences. Luc's new suitcase with useless-in-the-woods wheels screamed "clueless!" While Rick's sturdy, practical duffel bag didn't bother to say anything 'cause it didn't give a shit. But to be fair, he had thought they would be staying in a motel. While searching the Internet, he had found plenty of semi-civilized hotels and motels situated along the highway.

*Damn.* So far, he had succeeded in catching Rick's attention for all the wrong reasons.

Still, after a disastrous start to the day, Rick's apology and offer of a choice of rooms had eased the tension. The slight softening of Rick's attitude, that minor crack in his defensive armor was a good sign and gave Luc something to work with.

After dragging the bags from the truck, he turned toward the forest—Rick's domain. How many times had he pictured himself with Rick in a scene such as this? Of course, in his fantasies, his discord with nature was strangely absent. In his dreams, there were no bugs or critters in sight, and Rick had fallen head over heels in lust and couldn't wait to grab his office boy by the tie, drag him into the forest, and pin him against a surprisingly smooth and comfortable tree trunk to—

The cabin door swung open, and Rick strode down the wooden steps to stand by the front of the truck. Without his jacket, all six foot four inches or so of brawny man were on display. Muscles rippled beneath a tight gray T-shirt as he raised his arm and displayed an ax. "I'm going to chop wood."

Every drop of moisture disappeared from Luc's mouth. The desire to rip that T-shirt off and trace Rick's abs with his tongue made him a little shaky. "O-okay. Chop wood. Fire. Okay. Sure." Desperate to generate saliva in his arid mouth, he swallowed a few times as his gaze traced the hard muscles and curves clearly defined by the T-shirt. From the waistband of Rick's blue jeans (he didn't dare let his gaze drop below) upward past a sexy as hell six-pack, over the bumps and ridges of ribs before grazing across rock-hard pecs with tightly pebbled nipples. The muscles in Rick's corded neck twitched as Luc's gaze continued upward, over the close-cropped bristles framing an eminently kissable mouth.

He drew in a deep breath and focused on Rick's face. Brown eyes stared back at him. *Crap!* Rick had caught him ogling. How long had he been openly salivating over the man's delicious body?

Rick opened and then closed his mouth again without speaking before striding, ax in hand, toward the side of the cabin.

Luc stood transfixed, his attention never wavering from the sexy surveyor-slash-woodsman and the stretch of denim across Rick's ass. *Oh, yeah!* Lumberjack fantasies proved nothing compared to the real thing. As Rick rounded the corner of the cabin and strode from sight, Luc bounded up the porch steps and into the cabin. With a couple of heaves, the bags landed in their respective rooms, and he raced to the tiny kitchen window, hoping to catch a glimpse of Rick chopping wood. That particular fantasy, one of many scenarios, had kept him awake at night.

Yep. The window afforded a great view.

*Thwack.* With an easy, smooth swing, the ax sliced through the first chunk of wood.

*Thwack. THWACK.* The second impact sent a quiver through his gut as the stubborn piece yielded to Rick's strong stroke. Denim hugged Rick's ass as he bent to retrieve the split wood before tossing the wedges into a rectangular wire basket. *Clonk.*

Biceps. *Thwack.* Shoulders. *Thwack.* Ass. *Clonk.* The scene was everything Luc had envisaged. The only possible way to improve the scene would be if Rick removed his shirt.

*Please.*

*Thwack. Thwack. Clonk.*

Luc's groin reacted to each sound—especially the *clonk.*

*The man has a very fine ass.*

With the wood basket full, Rick embedded the ax in the chopping block and hefted the basket onto his shoulder. *Wow! And majorly strong.* Not wanting to get caught staring—gawking like a voyeur—he jumped away from the window and sighed. A shame about Rick's shirt staying on, but—

Rick shouldered the cabin door open and moved to the hearth. "There should be enough wood for tonight, but I'll have to chop more tomorrow. It gets chilly at night."

"Great!"

Rick's eyebrows shot upward at Luc's overly enthusiastic reply.

Heat crept up Luc's neck. "I-I mean, okay. I'll help you tomorrow."

Rick wiped his hands on his thighs. "Thanks, that'd be good."

"Yeah. Sure." Luc bit his lip to keep from grinning. With any luck, tomorrow would be hot. And sweaty.

*A guy can hope.*

Luc wandered over to the dining table and sat on the chair facing the fireplace. While mildly interested in the process of lighting the fire, he actually just wanted to watch Rick. The big man knelt on the hearth and arranged kindling in the fire grate, his movements smooth and confident. As Rick reached toward the metal basket and grabbed another piece of wood, Luc's focus shifted from Rick's large, capable hands to his ass.

The man had *qualities*.

Rick twisted around to face Luc. "Could you—?"

"What?" Startled, he locked in eye contact as his cheeks burned. *Shit.* Had Rick caught him ogling his ass?

"Could you turn the oven on? I bought a lasagna for tonight's meal. We'll have what you brought tomorrow night."

"Yeah, okay. Sure." He sprang from his seat and crossed the kitchen to study the various dials and knobs for a few seconds before turning the correct ones, conscious of Rick watching his every movement. Was Rick checking him out or wondering what had made his cabinmate so skittish?

The rasp of a match striking signaled an end to the uncomfortable scrutiny. As he turned toward Rick and the fireplace, the kindling caught alight. In less than a minute, the fire had taken hold, the flames engulfing the newly split logs.

Yes, the man had skills.

Rick rose from the hearth and placed the mesh fireguard in front of the blaze. "All set."

"Yeah, I'm guessing that's not your first fire."

Rick looked at his hands and then brushed them together. "No. Practice makes perfect."

Before Luc could respond, Rick had entered the kitchen, his massive presence dwarfing the area. Making Luc feel...small. His breaths became shallow as Rick took another step toward him, crowding him with his back against the sink. Heart pounding, he tipped his head and stared up at Rick. The man's chest was within touching distance, his mouth within kissing range. Were his fantasies about to come true?

Rick's gaze dipped to Luc's mouth. "I need to—"

"Yes." He placed his hand on Rick's hard chest. *Yes, please!*

"—wash my hands."

"Oh! Sure." As if his hand had caught on fire, he snatched it from Rick's chest and ducked sideways, sliding away from temptation. *Idiot.* He flexed his tingling hand before opening the fridge and staring blindly at the contents, hoping the chilled air would cool his burning face and neck.

*Imbecile.*

Water gushed from the kitchen tap as Rick washed his hands. "Lasagna's on the top shelf."

"Ah, yeah. Thanks." He took his time retrieving the store-bought lasagna, allowing the cold air to caress his hot cheeks for a few more seconds. His heart rate had almost returned to normal by the time he placed the container on the bench top.

Rick shut the water off. "Pass me the dishcloth?"

"Sure." While he handed over the cloth, a quick peek at Rick's face eased his mind and embarrassment. No grin, no smirk, and nothing to indicate ridicule. Maybe Rick hadn't realized.

*The sexual tension is obviously all in my own head. Moron.*

"S-so, is there anything I can do to help with dinner?"

"No. Thanks."

"Okay." He jiggled his knee. Should he stay in the kitchen? If not, what should he do?

After Rick placed the foil container in the oven and closed the door, they stared at each other for what seemed like a whole minute.

Rick broke the silence. "Shower or sit by the fire."

"Umm." While his sluggish brain tried to decipher the words, he gazed blankly at Rick.

"While the food cooks, you can take a shower or sit by the fire."

"Oh, okay. Yeah, I-I'll shower. Thanks." Grateful for the excuse to flee Rick's unsettling presence, Luc almost ran to his room and slammed the door. With a groan, he slumped onto the bed and put his head in his hands. Shit. Rick Masters was a very difficult man to read. And his clipped, three-word sentences were not helping. They gave no clue to what the man thought of him.

*Am I the only one embarrassed and confused?*

In that moment beside the sink, he could have sworn Rick had stared at his mouth as if he wanted to kiss him. With a sigh, he opened his suitcase on the bed and removed his toiletries bag and a clean shirt. He would just have to wait and see.

*And hope I don't make a total fool of myself.*

# Chapter Four

*"GODDAMN IT!"*

Rick smothered a smile. He had lost count of the "Goddamn its," "shits," and his personal favorite, "holy mother of hell," curses coming from the man behind him. Luc had to be the most accident-prone individual he had ever met. The level of injury appeared to denote which particular curse he used. "Goddamn it" seemed to signify stinging pain, a minor amount of blood, and frustrated embarrassment.

Rick stopped and looked behind.

Red-faced, Luc brushed his hand on his jeans before inspecting the new wound. "It's fine. Keep going."

"Is it bleeding?" Rick retraced his steps to Luc's side.

Luc's brow furrowed and his bottom lip protruded. "No."

"Liar." He grabbed Luc's hand and turned it palm up to expose the raw scrapes. "Come on; sit on that rock while I clean and bandage it. I need to—"

"Yeah, yeah. You want to minimize the chance of infection. I know the drill. You've told me three times already." Luc held up his bandaged right thumb. "One." Raised his bruised and scraped left elbow. "Two." Then he indicated the tear in the black denim over his right knee, exposing a white bandage. "Three." Luc huffed. "I get it. We have to keep them clean so they don't get infected by God knows what here in the beautiful friggin' wonder of nature."

Rick's mouth twitched. The urge to suck on Luc's bordering-on-pouty bottom lip was seriously strong. Instead, he used his size to crowd the smaller man and force him backward to a large rock.

He curled his hand around Luc's bicep. *Nice muscle tone. Not too big, and not too small.*

Luc was not his usual type. He had always preferred his men to be brawny and robust—men who thrived in the tough outdoors and matched him in size and weight. Not that anyone could call Luc puny or small, but he definitely fell into the category of "regular build."

An image of Luc, shirtless, flashed into his mind. A year ago, one brief glimpse of Luc's flesh in the men's locker room had fueled his fantasies for weeks. Months. Okay, he would admit that they hadn't really stopped. A particularly compelling scenario involved the removal of Luc's shirt and tie. With the shirt relegated to the floor, the tie was used in a very imaginative way to display Luc's body.

"Regular" could be pretty darn appealing.

But of course, Luc was also the boss's nephew, so... No.

He drew in a deep breath and pushed Luc down onto the rock. "Sit."

The lip protruded a little more. "Yes, sir, Mr. Masters."

Rick's cock twitched. *Damn.* That sarcastic comment combined with a very tempting, pouty lip... One side of his mouth curved upward. "Just 'Sir' will do, or if you prefer, 'Master.'"

Luc's head snapped back fast enough to cause whiplash, and wide, startled eyes stared. "What?" Luc's Adam's apple bobbed as he swallowed. Hard. "I, umm."

Rick grinned and retrieved the first aid kit from his backpack. "Okay, give me your hand." Luc's gaze slid away, and silence descended as Rick cleansed and taped the wound. First aid probably wasn't necessary as the scrape wasn't particularly bad, but he had to admit he liked having an excuse to touch Luc.

As Luc kept his eyes averted and ducked his head, the sun's rays filtered through the trees, stretching out to caress his hair. Had Luc freaked out with the "Sir" and "Master" comment? He had been joking—mostly. He stifled the urge to raise Luc's head and stare into his arresting green eyes. He wanted to run his fingers through that blond hair, and grip and guide Luc's head as he thrust into Luc's mou—

*Oh, God.* His cock hardened and his heart pounded. *Okay, calm down. No need to act like a caveman and prove the "someone like you" comment.* He drew in a deep breath and smoothed down the final edge of the bandage. "There, all done."

"Thanks." Luc avoided eye contact. "Now can we get on with the job? How many more coordinates do we need to locate?"

Rick took a step backward and stared at Luc. When Luc had first uttered *that* comment, it had made him angry. Sure, most people would think him a bit rough when compared to those who worked in an office, with their silk shirts, ties, and tongues. In his line of work, he had no need or care for such things, but still the statement stung. He had thought Luc was judging him—declaring him inferior.

But seeing Luc like this. Damn it, he didn't know what to think. Maybe he had misjudged Luc.

*Or am I just trying to convince myself because I want him?*

With a sigh, he pulled the GPS from his backpack and switched it on. The screen flickered for a few moments before clearing. "Five more. Should be able to finish by midafternoon."

Luc snorted. "Yeah, sure, if I suddenly transform into a competent human being and help, instead of hinder you. Honestly, I told my uncle he shouldn't send me on this job-swap program. If they had sent my friend Adam you'd have been finished already, and the first aid kit would be untouched."

"What's so great about this guy Adam?"

"Well, for starters, he camps, hikes, and rock climbs. I can guarantee his hiking boots wouldn't be brand-new and chafing the hell out of his feet. Adam wouldn't get blisters the size of eggs."

He directed his gaze to Luc's boots. "You have blisters? Why didn't you say so?"

Luc groaned. "Okay. Forget I said anything. I sound like the biggest whiny wuss on the planet."

Rick smiled. He didn't want to like Luc, but it was becoming increasingly difficult to remain aloof. The sting of the "someone like you" comment faded with each of Luc's self-deprecating remarks. With each awkward accident, the sight of Luc's red face melted his resolve to keep things polite and professional. In the office environment, Luc appeared confident, sexy, and self-assured, or so it seemed when watching him from afar, but in the great outdoors, Luc was clumsy and...endearing. "Okay, I won't ask about the blisters again, but promise me you'll say if you need to stop and apply a Band-Aid to them."

Luc nodded. "Yeah, yeah, sure." Still seated on the rock, he leaned down to pick up his water bottle. "Now let's go and—what the fuck?" Luc sprang from the rock and flew to Rick's side. "Fuck! The little fucker bit me." Luc grimaced and flicked his hand. "Did you see that? What was that? Fuck!"

Laughter rumbled in Rick's chest. He couldn't help it. The expression on Luc's face was priceless!

While continuing to flick and shake his injured hand, Luc looked up at him. "What the hell? Did you see the size of that thing? It was huge. It could have rabies or something."

Biting his lip to stifle the laughter, he grabbed Luc's hand to inspect yet another injury. "Mmm, not good. From the bite pattern, it was probably a—"

"What? What the hell was it?"

"Unfortunately, I believe it was a rabid—"

"Oh, God!"

"A rabid, killer squirrel."

Luc's mouth hung open for a second before he snatched his hand away. "Ha, ha. Very funny."

The smile Rick had been trying to suppress burst forth. "You should have seen the look on your face."

Luc scowled for a moment before his brow smoothed and the edges of his mouth curled upward. "Yeah, Okay. I'm not usually such a drama queen. Or a klutz. Or a wuss. Shit. This nature trip is so not good for the ego."

Rick chuckled and retrieved the first aid kit. Again. "Come on, then; you know the drill."

"Yeah, yeah."

After another round of antiseptic application, they headed northeast toward the next coordinate point. Rick traversed the terrain with agility and ease.

*This is what I do—who I am.*

Over the years, he had struggled to find his place in the world. A gangly giant by the age of fifteen, he had towered over classmates and teachers alike. Add in a severe lack of coordination and fitting in had never been an option. It wasn't until the age of eighteen, on his first hiking trip, that he had discovered the environment had been contributing to his clumsiness. In the great outdoors, there were no doorframes to duck under, no flimsy chairs designed for people a foot shorter than him, or stair treads too small for his feet.

And no china or glass.

Nature let him breathe.

Of course, over the years, his physique had filled out, and he had learned to control his body in all environments, but a man of his size would never quite fit in a world made for the "average" person.

Yet, unlike the city environment, nature never made him feel like a giant Neanderthal. Instead, it made him happy, comfortable, and content. He loved the fresh scents of nature, the sounds of birds and animals, the wind sneaking through tree branches, and the—

Strangled scream of pain from the man behind him.

He spun around. Luc lay crumpled on the path, holding his ankle and biting his lip. A twisted ankle? He hurried back to Luc and knelt beside him. "Is it bad?"

Luc grimaced and nodded.

It appeared Luc's silence, not curses, denoted major pain. He unlaced Luc's hiking boot, eased it from his foot, and peeled the sock away. Other than a small hiss, Luc made no sound and kept his head lowered. The ankle had already swelled, and blood had begun to pool under the skin. "Damn. That must be painful."

"Mmm."

Rick gently lowered Luc's foot to the ground. "I have a cold pack in my bag." He opened his backpack and removed the pliable ice pack wrapped around his water bottle. "It's no longer frozen, but at least it's cool." Pressing the blue gel pack to the outside of Luc's ankle, he noted the angry, weeping blister on Luc's heel, the tension in his body, and the unnatural pallor of his face. "Are you going to pass out?"

"I-I don't think so. God, I hope not." Luc groaned. "That's all I need. This is already the worst experience of my life."

Rick bit back a smile. "Don't talk too soon. We still need to hike back to the cabin." He had not thought it possible, but Luc's face paled further.

"Shit. I-I don't know how I'll..." Luc drew in a deep breath. "Okay, help me up and I'll lean on you and hop. I guess."

He pulled Luc to his feet—or foot—and gripped his biceps as Luc swayed backward, his eyes glazed and unfocused. "Stay with me, Luc. Come on, buddy, you're going to be okay."

Luc groaned. "No, I don't...think I am."

As Luc's body slumped, limp and heavy, Rick wrapped his arms around him, anchored him close to his chest, and lifted, careful to keep any weight from Luc's foot. No way could Luc walk or hop to the cabin, and only one solution came to mind.

"Hey! Luc! Buddy!"

Luc's head lolled, and he moaned as he came to again. "Wha-what happened?"

"You passed out."

"Noooo. No, I'mmma real man. I swear."

He smiled at the slurred words. "Don't worry about it; of course you are."

Luc blinked. "What?" He tilted his head to stare up at Rick. "What are you doing?"

"You passed out from the pain in your ankle."

"Oh, shit, 'cause that's not embarrassing."

He chuckled and shifted his hold. "I'm going to carry you back to the cabin."

"What? No way!" Luc wriggled, trying to break free of Rick's bear hug. "I'm not some delicate flower who needs the big, sexy hero to rescue me and carry me home."

Rick leaned close, his lips almost touching Luc's ear. "Does that make me the 'big, sexy hero'?"

Luc gasped and ceased struggling. "No, I-I didn't mean that."

Rick laughed. "Well, I will have to rescue you. Brace yourself."

"What?"

With a quick maneuver, before Luc had a chance to do more than squawk, he hoisted Luc over his shoulder in a fireman's lift.

Upside down, Luc flailed about for a second, no doubt trying to get his bearings, and then huffed before lying still. Luc groaned and his muffled voice broke. "Thi-this is not real. I'll wake up soon in my apartment and realize this was just a horrible nightmare. No need to be embarrassed—this trip never happened. No scrapes, no twisted ankles, no mind-numbing embarrassment from fainting and being slung over..."

Rick smiled as the monologue continued. He quite enjoyed the *bump, bump* of Luc's head—or chin—as it knocked against his ass in sync with his stride. Although, he didn't think that was supposed to happen, so perhaps it wasn't the perfect fireman's hold. Probably more of a basic caveman tactic. Sling the stunned, disorientated guy over your shoulder and drag him home to the cave, or in this case, cabin. And then...

*It's a pity I can't do* that.

He grinned and strode toward the cabin. Despite Luc's grumbling and discontented words, a flush of warmth filled Rick's chest. This need to care for and *take control* was new to him. Manhandling Luc sure felt good. Yep, he had Luc Weston exactly where he wanted him.

*Although, under me would be even better. Damn. Must remember he's the boss's nephew.*

After five minutes, Luc's monologue mumblings were still in full swing. The guy sure knew some colorful curse words. Rick bounced, hitching Luc back into position over his shoulder. In an effort to hold Luc in place, he shifted his hand higher on Luc's leg, his fingers brushing Luc's inner thigh.

Luc's breath hitched and the words ceased.

Well, he appeared to have found a very enjoyable way to render Luc speechless.

He inched his fingers higher.

*I wonder if I can make him squawk again.*

# Chapter Five

HOLY MOTHER OF hell, his ankle hurt!

Luc limped across the small kitchen to the sink. Of all the stupid, embarrassing things to do! The morning had been bad enough with all the scrapes and cuts, but his embarrassment had skyrocketed when he had tripped and twisted an ankle—and then been carried home over Rick's shoulder.

*Rick must think I'm a total loser.*

After turning on the tap, he carefully directed the flow of water across the uncovered sections of his hands, trying to keep the bandages dry. The "killer squirrel" bite—or whatever the hell that critter was—still stung like the devil. God, talk about pathetic. He needed to go home, back to the city where he didn't need rescuing every five minutes. Although, as embarrassing as it was to be carried over Rick's shoulders, it was also kind of hot. Along with the heavy dose of mortification, he'd had a few stray thoughts of bears and lairs.

And what might happen when they arrived at the cabin.

The front door opened.

A sharp pain speared through his ankle as he spun toward the door, and air hissed through his clenched teeth. *Stupid ankle.*

Rick dumped his backpack on the table and frowned. "I thought you were going to rest that ankle while I finished the survey."

"I did. I lay on the couch all afternoon. I only just got up to make a salad for dinner." He gestured to the bowl of salad on the countertop.

An earthy forest scent, overlaid by manly lumberjack, enveloped him as Rick moved closer. Peering into the bowl, Rick raised an eyebrow. "Salad?"

Luc's heart started jumping crazily as a muscled arm brushed against his chest. "I-I brought steaks and baked potatoes too."

Rick's eyebrow lowered. "Ah, good. For a moment, I thought you were expecting me to be satisfied with rabbit food. It takes more than a bit of green stuff to fuel a body this size."

Luc's eyes zeroed in on the hard pectoral muscles covered by a thin, sweat-dampened blue T-shirt. He flexed his fingers as he fought the urge to touch the hard—

"Do I have time for a shower before dinner? I'm sweaty."

Luc focused on the bead of sweat trailing down Rick's neck. "Yes, I like it."

"Pardon?"

"Umm, what?" *Crap! Did I just say 'I like it?'*

Rick frowned. "So, I'll get a quick shower then?"

"Yeah, sure." Heat crept up his neck and over his cheeks. *Crap!* Was he intent on completely embarrassing himself?

A flash of movement and skin brought his focus to Rick's back as he departed. With one jerk, the blue T-shirt was whipped over Rick's head to reveal tanned, taut skin.

The bathroom door closed, blocking the rippling shoulder muscles from his view. *Damn!* His heart raced. On the other side of that door, Rick would be unfastening his jeans and dropping them to the floor.

The sound of water rushing through the pipes echoed throughout the cabin.

On the other side of that door, Rick would soon be naked, his big hands slowly spreading soap over his big, naked body. Sliding, stroking, and gripping. *Big. Naked.* He could not get those two words out of his head. Was Rick *big* all over?

Luc's cock stirred, hardening and pushing against the constraint of his jeans. *God! Calm down.* Between the bad first impression and the pathetic injuries, he didn't stand a chance.

Or did he? Rick had become a little too familiar with Luc's inner thigh on the way home. On purpose?

No. No, despite Rick's apparent ease, not to mention his unfaltering, strong stride, it would be difficult to carry a grown man for such a long distance. Rick would have needed to shift his hold multiple times. The fact that Rick had held him high on his thigh, and then his fingers had grazed his... Well, that was probably an accident. Both times.

It probably didn't mean anything.

But it didn't stop him from hoping.

When Rick returned from showering—an image he kept returning to—they ate dinner but remained mostly silent. Lost in his own thoughts, Rick seemed content with only minor conversation about the day's activities.

After dinner, Luc settled at one end of the couch, cradling a mug of coffee between his hands. The fire crackled, casting a soft orange glow over the room. He swallowed as Rick maneuvered his large frame onto the seat beside him, his long legs stretched out toward the fire. A thigh encased in denim brushed against Luc's leg, sending quivers through his belly. Suddenly the couch seemed very small. No need for a fire—the heat emanating from Rick's body could warm the entire cabin.

Rick shifted, crossing his outstretched legs at the ankles. "Dinner was good."

"Thanks."

"I liked the sauce stuff you put on the rabbit food."

"Thanks. It's just a store-bought salad dressing."

"Still, it was good."

The fire hissed and popped.

The old clock on the mantelpiece ticked loudly.

Luc bit his lip. He needed to say something. He started jiggling his leg. Ask him something. Anything. His eyes searched the cozy cabin for inspiration. The dim lights and roaring fire created an intimate setting. Which was all wrong because right at that moment, they were merely two acquaintances on a couch with a pile of awkwardness between them. During their hike, Rick had surprised him by gradually speaking more; his initial one-word answers had become two, then three, and finally full sentences. He hoped they hadn't reverted to square one.

A warm hand curled over his leg an inch above his knee and pressed down, quelling the agitated movement. His breath caught. What was this, then? His focus slid from Luc's hand to meet an intense brown-eyed stare.

Rick's tongue snaked out, moistening his lips before he spoke. "I think we got off to a bad start yesterday. What do you say we put yesterday behind us and start over? Today was good. Well," Rick's mouth twisted, "apart from all the scrapes and injuries."

The big hand on Luc's leg gave a gentle squeeze. Heat rushed up his leg and headed on a direct course to his groin. Not trusting his vocal chords, Luc nodded. Hyperaware of Rick's hand and each miniscule twitch of Rick's fingers against his leg, he forced himself to breathe slowly as his heart rate rose another notch.

*What did this mean?*

Aside from the whole fireman's lift thing, placing a hand on another man's leg, not to mention keeping it there, was not your everyday friendly gesture.

Luc worried his bottom lip with his teeth and focused on Rick's hand again. Long, strong fingers moved, skimming the inside of his knee, sending tiny sparks of pleasure across his thigh. His heart bashed against his ribs, and a bead of sweat rolled down his temple. Over the last few minutes, the temperature of the cabin had skyrocketed, and it had nothing to do with the fire in the stone fireplace. "So!" His voice squeaked. *What the hell?* He cleared his throat. "So, Rick, do you come here often?" *Shit! Stupid, stupid, stupid.* "I mean, how many times have you stayed in this cabin?"

"I'm not sure. I've lost count. It's a good central base. So far, I've plotted the boundary coordinates for a few reserves to the north and some between here and White River National Park. It's tough, rugged terrain, so the comfort of the cabin after a hard day's trek is appreciated. Some survey trips are far less civilized, and I have to take the tent or sleep in the truck."

"Geez, that sounds horrible." *And that was one massively long speech from the big guy.*

"No, I don't mind roughing it that much. As you can see, I'm built for the tough life."

"Yeah." Luc's eyes focused on the pectoral muscles, clearly defined by Rick's gray T-shirt. His fingers itched to burrow under the fabric and splay across the hard flesh. His gaze slid higher to the close-cropped beard. "Like a bear." He blinked. "Shit! Did I just say that out loud?"

A deep chuckle rolled through Rick's chest. "Yes. You did."

"Oh, God. Sorry. That was stupid. I think I've said and done more stupid things in the last two days than I have in...well, a long time."

"So, by 'stupid,' you mean the tripping and stumbling."

"Yeah."

"And the lack of filter between your brain and your mouth."

Luc grimaced. "Yep."

A slow smile spread across Rick's lips. "You know, each time you do or say something..."

"Stupid."

Rick chuckled. "Yes. I think it makes me..." He shook his head. "Never mind."

"What?" Luc's heart raced. *Makes him what? Makes him realize what an idiot I am? Makes him want to laugh at me? Makes him wish he was here with a real man?*

"Nothing." Rick leaned in close. "Forget it."

Luc's chest grew tight as Rick's breath whispered across his cheek. *What the...?* His attention zeroed in on Rick's mouth. Well, Rick definitely wasn't laughing at him now. The distance between them disappeared as Rick leaned closer and pressed a chaste kiss to his mouth before nibbling on his lip. Luc gasped. *Holy...* Definitely unexpected, but he liked it. A lot.

Bristles tickled his face, sending shivery flutters down through his belly. Soft. Rick's close-cropped beard was softer than he had thought it would be. He tipped his head and rubbed his cheek against the dark fur—beard. Against Rick's beard.

*I must stop thinking about bears.*

The hints of coffee and manly musk, the tickle of bristles, and the light scrape of teeth all combined to seduce and leave him wanting more. With a needy groan that embarrassingly sounded like a whimper, Luc leaned forward, chasing Rick's mouth. He wanted a real taste. Needed a real kiss. Another whimper escaped his lips as Rick pulled away.

Rick removed his hand from Luc's leg and stood up. "That was..." He frowned and shook his head. "Sorry. I shouldn't... Do you want...?"

The blood pounded through Luc's head as a big, callused hand reached out toward him, palm up. Waiting. *Do I want...to let him wrap me in his strong arms? To kiss me senseless? To go to the bedroom with him? Hell, yes!* He placed his hand in Rick's.

Rick's mouth twitched. "Err, I meant for you to pass me your coffee cup."

"Huh?"

"Your coffee cup. I asked if you want another coffee."

Luc snatched his hand back. *Idiot.* Heat raced up his neck and scorched his cheeks. "No, no thanks."

"Okay then." Rick walked the few steps to the kitchen as if nothing had happened.

*What the hell?* Luc's gut churned as he scrambled to his feet. Rick had kissed him and then pulled away—*as if nothing had happened.* Should he say something? Confront him?

*And say what? Come back? Kiss me again?*

No. There had been enough self-humiliation for one day. "I-I think I'll go to bed." As he limped across the room, each painful step stung his flesh and pride. Midway, the deep rumble of Rick's voice froze him to the spot.

"I'll have another coffee and then follow you to bed."

Luc swiveled his head to gape at Rick. Did he mean his bed? Together?

Rick stared. "I'll see you in the morning."

The heat in Luc's cheeks blazed out of control as he fumbled with the doorknob. "Right. Good night." After he had scrambled into the bedroom, the door slammed behind him with a thud, the thick wood muffling Rick's reply.

Closing his eyes, he slumped against the door. Okay, so that had been embarrassing, and yet, the big man's contradictory actions were difficult to decipher. Rick had flirted with him and kissed him, so perhaps he had a chance with the sexy lumberjack after all.

# Chapter Six

LUC GROANED AND opened his eyes to stare at the ceiling. A choir of birds chirped and warbled outside the cabin window. He had been dreaming about them. While he lay on a forest path, immobile with a twisted ankle, a swarm of horrible little black-and-white birds had flown around him, swooping and squawking—taunting him. He had waited for someone to rescue him, but Rick never showed.

A shrill screech cut through the medley of forest sounds, sending a spear of pain through Luc's temples and dragging him back to the present. Birds. Rotten fuckers.

*I hate nature.*

With an embarrassingly strangled groan, he swung his legs over the side of the bed and rolled to a seated position. Neck, arms, ribs, hips, ass—everything ached.

He stood up. "Ahhh!" Agony. Pure agony sliced through his ankle like...like knives. Lame analogy, but it was the best his pain-shocked brain could conjure.

The bedroom door slammed open, and Rick's massive frame filled the doorway. "Luc? You screamed. Are you okay?"

Luc swayed, his vision blurring, before the pain gradually subsided. His temples pulsated in time with the throbbing of his ankle. "Yep. I just need a minute." He curled his hand around the wooden bedpost—just in case. *And I didn't scream, I yelled. Little girls scream. Grown men yell.* With his shaky legs threatening to crumple, he sank down and perched on the edge of the mattress. "My ankle is a bit painful this morning. Sorry if I woke you."

Rick grinned. "It's 8:00 a.m. I've been up for two hours."

He groaned. "Of course you have."

"Do you need help? I can assist you to the bathroom if you want. I can see it's not only your ankle." He frowned and gestured toward Luc's hip and ribs. "You look like someone beat you up."

Luc stared down at the gray-and-purple bruise covering his left hip. When he had twisted his ankle, his left hip had taken the brunt of the fall—his currently bare left hip, bare side, and chest. *Shit*. Heat rose, spreading over his chest and heading to his cheeks. Wearing only low-slung white boxer shorts, he may as well have been naked. Rick's intense inspection of his exposed body fanned the flames until Luc feared his pale skin must be glowing.

He glanced down at his chest. Yep, there it was. Mottled, fire-engine-red skin. He cleared his throat, praying his voice wouldn't squeak. "No. No, thanks. I can make it to the bathroom on my own."

Rick nodded. "Okay, when you're done, we'll have a quick breakfast and then head home."

"Yeah, sure. Thanks."

"Okay then." Rick's lingering gaze scorched a trail over Luc's chest, stomach, and...

Luc resisted the urge to cover his groin with his hands.

With a sharp nod, Rick backed out of the room. "Call me if you need anything."

The door closed with a soft thud.

Luc drew in a deep breath. If that was his reaction to Rick merely looking at his body, what would happen if Rick touched him?

*And I definitely want Rick to touch me.*

The night before, that barely there kiss and the gentle nibbling on his bottom lip hadn't been nearly enough. He wanted more. A scoff escaped his lips. Fat chance of that if he kept embarrassing himself by being a klutz. Or being so crazy in lust that he mistook "Can I get you another coffee?" for "Can I take you to bed and do unspeakable things to you?" Or turning red—all over—at a mere look. Closing his eyes, he groaned.

*Acting like a total loser is not going to get Rick's attention.*

Well, it was, but not in a good way.

Okay, enough of the self-pity, time to get moving. With a few hops and painful steps, he maneuvered around the bedroom, retrieving a change of clothes from his suitcase. A warm shower might have eased his aches and pains, but Rick seemed keen to depart, so Luc needed to make a quick visit to the bathroom to relieve himself and wash his face. However, running the gauntlet from bedroom to bathroom needed some planning. No way would he hop across the cabin's main room wearing only his boxers. His bits were sure to flip and flop about in an embarrassing display, and Rick had already received an eyeful of his barely covered junk.

Unfortunately, he had only brought two pairs of jeans— the pair he had worn the previous day (his favorites, now ruined by flailing around in the dirt) and the backup pair (old and a smidge too tight). They were going to be hellish to squeeze into with his bruises and scrapes.

After grabbing the backup jeans, he sat on the bed, and amid plenty of grunts and a few "ouches," he pulled and shimmied until the denim reached thigh level. Out of breath, he released a frustrated huff and flopped back against the mattress. Talk about hard work. In hindsight, bringing some looser pants would have been more practical. Obviously.

*Too focused on which pairs would tempt Rick to look at my ass.*

Okay, back to the task. He drew in a deep breath. The final maneuvers were bound to hurt his hip, but it had to be done. Arching his body, ass off the bed, he thrust his hips upward while yanking at the waistband of his jeans, punctuating each thrust and yank with his words: "Must. Stop. Thinking. With. My. Dick."

"Ah, sorry."

Luc whipped his head around and froze, mid groin-thrust, suspended in the air and disbelief.

*Of all the rotten timing and luck and embarrassing moments.*

Rick stood in the doorway staring, his focus fixed on Luc's boxer-clad dick. "I...sorry. I did knock, but you were obviously...distracted."

*Oh, shit.* In slow motion, Luc lowered his ass to the bed. If only he could keep sinking downward until the mattress swallowed him whole.

Rick cleared his throat. "I'd offer to help, but..."

"No! No thanks." Was that his voice or a cat being strangled?

"I'll... Breakfast." Rick waved his hand vaguely toward the kitchen before clearing his throat again. "I'll give you a few minutes to...finish." The big man spun on his heel and disappeared from sight.

*Shit. Shitshitshit.*

After a quick breakfast of toast and coffee, they packed their gear into the truck and headed out. Luc remained mostly silent as mixed emotions and thoughts swirled through his head. He was happy to leave the numerous incidents of gut-churning embarrassment behind, but as much as Luc hated the outdoors—and the incompetence that came with it—he was sad to drive away from the cabin. The cabin where Rick had kissed him.

The truck bounced and rocked as Rick drove slowly down the dirt track leading to the main road. As Luc fumbled the seat-belt buckle, he snuck a quick glance at Rick. A faint layer of sunburn-pink tinged Rick's nose. Judging by Rick's tanned neck and arms—and the hard, muscular back he had glimpsed the day before—the rosy hue would soon darken and blend into the golden skin. What he wouldn't give to touch that skin.

The truck jerked as the right front wheel hit a pothole. With the seat-belt buckle still in his hand and nothing to restrain him, Luc lurched forward and smacked his head on the dashboard. "Oh, holy mother of..." Stars danced before his eyes, or was it fireflies? No, it wasn't nighttime, was it?

"Luc? Buddy? Can you hear me?"

"Wha—?" He opened his eyes. "What?" He blinked, his eyes focusing on the black material beneath his cheek, covering hard pectoral muscles. A pleasant, earthy scent filled his senses. *Rick.* "What happened?" With a groan, he heaved his sluggish body upright and away from Rick's chest.

"You hit your head on the dashboard. My fault. I should have waited until you had your seat belt fastened. Are you okay now?"

"Yeah, yeah, sure." He fumbled with the seat belt again. It just wouldn't cooperate.

Strong hands batted his clumsy fingers away and took control, clicking the seat belt into position. "There." Rick brushed the hair away from Luc's forehead, his fingers lingering. "You'll probably have a goose egg by the time we get home."

"Great." His shoulders slumped and his forehead throbbed. It was official; without grass or rocks or animals to prove it, he was not built for the outdoors.

*I'm a disaster waiting to happen—even inside the truck.*

Beside him, Rick refastened his own seat belt and started the truck. Again. A slight smile appeared on Rick's face. "You need a keeper."

Luc bit his lip and stared out the window. What a trip! He had hoped they would map some reserve coordinates and spend time getting to know each other—see if it could lead to something...more. Instead, the map pointed a clear course to "Singlesville." No way would rugged Rick be interested in someone who "needed a keeper."

*God!* He hoped his incompetence wore off by the time they returned to civilization.

He sat up straighter. In the city, he could make a better impression. Without all those pesky, outdoorsy things to scrape and bite and trip him, he was certain to succeed. Well, at least not do any worse. The difficulty lay in getting together with Rick. They didn't precisely run in the same social circles. Surely, he could think of something.

Despite Rick's unreadable expression, the heavy shroud of failure lifted from Luc's shoulders. In the city, he could impress Rick with his charm and wit while surrounded by the familiar. Without unexpected encounters with flora or fauna to trip him up—so to speak.

He smiled and admired the lush scenery. Perhaps he still had a chance with Rick.

Technically, Thursday and Friday should be spent accompanying Rick on surveying jobs, but his twisted ankle wouldn't allow that. Most likely, he would return to the office for two days. There were a few low-priority survey plans waiting for amendment and completion. The week after, his ankle should be fine to resume surveying with Rick. Fingers crossed for some semi-civilized survey sites where he could impress the big guy by staying on his feet. And no blood would be a bonus.

*So, I need to show Rick that in my own environment, I possess other qualities.*

# Chapter Seven

ANOTHER MONDAY, ANOTHER survey. Rick maneuvered through the chaotic morning traffic, his tension eased by the laid-back music sneaking through the truck's speakers. Nothing like a bit of jazz to transform his mood. Despite being within the city limits, the next survey would be simple and relaxed. Unlike the man in the passenger seat. Beside him, Luc bounced and jiggled his denim-clad leg like a kangaroo on crack. Definitely not relaxed. At least Luc had had the sense to wear regular-fit blue jeans today. Those black skinny jeans from the first trip were entirely unsuitable. Not to mention distracting.

Luc's leg stopped moving. "So where's this survey located?"

"Not far."

After a short silence, Luc sighed, and the leg gymnastics resumed.

Rick preferred to limit conversation and drive through city traffic with the sound of great music to accompany and soothe him. A glance at Luc confirmed frowning and frantic lip biting. Was Luc still uncomfortable in his presence? He assumed they had passed that awkward stage and moved on to simmering sexual tension, but then again, his people-reading skills were crap. "We're surveying a small recreation reserve on the outskirts of Boulder."

"Oh, okay. So is it a GPS job, or will we use a Theodolite?"

With his eyebrow raised, he turned to stare at Luc for a few seconds.

"What?" Luc stared back.

"Nothing." He returned his attention to the road.

"Are you surprised I know the difference?"

"A bit."

Luc sat up straighter. "Well, I do."

"Good for you." He tried to suppress a grin, but Luc's tone had him imagining a "so there" attached to the end of Luc's statement. Very belligerent teenager. Of course, what he wanted to do to that pouty bottom lip could only be done to a fully grown man.

The leg jiggling continued as Luc mumbled something unintelligible.

"Stop!" Leaving one hand on the steering wheel, he clamped his other hand onto Luc's thigh. As the agitated movement ceased, the tense muscles and warmth beneath his palm proved an irresistible temptation. He edged his hand a little higher and squeezed.

Luc gasped and froze. "Wha-what?"

"That leg is distracting."

"Um, okay. Sorry. It's a nervous habit. I-I'll try to keep it still."

"Mmm." The muscles beneath his hand twitched, bringing to mind their trek through the forest, Luc slung over his shoulder, and his fingers grazing Luc's... *Damn.* He gave a short, sharp laugh as his cock stirred. "I doubt keeping it still will help."

"Pardon?"

"Never mind." He removed his hand from Luc's thigh and returned it to the steering wheel. Keeping his hands to himself was proving more difficult than he had anticipated. Immediately after their brief but memorable kiss by the fireside, Rick had struggled with the benefits of proceeding and the logical decision to keep his hands off Luc. Common sense won, and he had managed to put an end to what would surely have culminated in him slinging Luc over his shoulder and carting him off to the bedroom.

But it had been a close call. Very close.

And thoughts of all the various ways he could manhandle Luc had kept him awake that night.

And every night since.

Rick parked the truck beside a grassy area. Groups of trees and a small pond added to the picture of a pretty recreation reserve. "This is it. It's a basic, clear-view site. We'll use the Theodolite."

"Okay, sure."

"How's the ankle?"

"A little sore still, but I can do the job."

"Okay, I'm glad it's better. Let me know if you need to give it a rest." He swept his gaze over Luc from head to toe. Truthfully, although he'd never want Luc to be in pain, he wouldn't mind locking Luc's arms around his neck and carrying him from each peg to the next position. Of course, only if Luc's ankle hurt; otherwise, it would just be awkward. Maybe slightly creepy.

*But it would be totally acceptable and sexy in the bedroom—or on the way to the shower.*

*Yes, it would definitely be sexy carrying Luc to the shower.*

*Focus!* He drew in a deep breath. "Okay. Let's get started."

Luc attempted to exit the truck, but his body jerked as the still-fastened seat belt halted his progress. In an instant, Luc's neck and face turned pink.

Rick's mouth twitched as he suppressed a smile and stared, fascinated by the rosy flush of color.

"Shit." Luc fumbled with the seat-belt clasp. "Shitshitshit."

"Hey." Rick reached over and grasped a slim wrist in each of his hands. He closed his fingers in a firm grip, his thumb and forefinger completing the circles like a pair of restraints—like handcuffs. An image flashed through his mind of Luc spread-eagled and handcuffed to the bed—his bed. His cock swelled, and a growly groan escaped his lips.

Luc gasped, his startled stare locking onto Rick.

Rick stared back, his hold instinctively tightening for a second before he released Luc and then the seat-belt buckle. He watched Luc scramble and almost fall from the truck. Damn. He needed a moment to calm down. Everything Luc did, every action and reaction, made him horny as hell. Lip biting, leg jiggling, fumbling, and rosy-red skin flushing had never turned him on before. But on Luc, those things looked mighty sexy.

Okay. He needed to focus on work—surveying. Exiting the vehicle, he slammed the truck door on his thoughts. "Okay, let's unload the gear."

The morning passed quickly, and despite his ambiguous feelings on the matter, Luc's ankle stayed strong, eliminating the need for heroics. He'd had to give himself a few stern warnings about staring at Luc's ass, but overall, he had managed to stay professional. The survey had gone well with Luc proving both helpful and knowledgeable in the use of a Theodolite, and by midafternoon, they were back in the truck and heading for the office. With the last survey scheduled for the week completed, their official time together had ended. His mouth turned down. He had grown accustomed to Luc's company.

*Now I'll be lucky to catch a glimpse of him around the office. Still, it's probably for the best.*

"You did well today. A great help."

"Thanks." Luc smiled and bit his lip.

"We make a good team."

"Yeah."

Luc appeared pleased by the praise, and that smile gave Rick tingles in unmentionable places. "So, how was your time as an apprentice surveyor?"

"I guess I'll let you know at the end of the week."

"No, that's our last one."

"What?" Luc spun around to look at him. "What do you mean?"

"I don't have any more scheduled until next week. So you're off the hook."

"Oh, shit." Luc frowned before turning away.

"I thought you'd be happy."

"Well, yeah, but... Shit."

They lapsed into silence, Luc staring out the window and Rick concentrating on driving, both allowing the music to fill the gap. Rick wasn't sure what to make of Luc's reaction.

"So, Rick." Luc raised his voice to speak over the music, glanced at him, and then returned his focus to the passing traffic. "Most of the cartography crowd gets together on Fridays after work at DuPont's. I've seen a few surveyors there. Tony and... I think his name is Jack?"

"Yes. Jack Dawson. He's a good friend."

"Oh, yeah, Jack Dawson. I recognize that name from his field books. It's good to put a face to the name." Luc grimaced and jiggled his leg for a few seconds before ceasing the action. "So, maybe I'll see you sometime at DuPont's? You know, if you're there with Jack and Tony." Luc bit back a groan.

Rick kept his eyes fixed on the road. "Mmm, maybe. If I'm free." Warmth flooded his chest at Luc's adorably transparent ploy. Luc wanted to see him again.

He suppressed a smile.

*Roll on Friday night.*

# Chapter Eight

LUC TAPPED HIS pen on the desk. "I can't believe it's only Wednesday. This week is dragging so bad."

Adam Anderson pushed a stack of survey plans aside and perched on the edge of Luc's desk. "It only feels slow because you're all tied up in knots over Rick. Honestly, if I catch you sighing and staring off into space one more time, I'll steal your phone and text him myself."

"What? Shit no!"

"I don't get why you won't just ask him outright if he'll go to DuPont's with you on Friday?"

Luc's focus darted to his right; to the place he usually kept his mobile phone. Still there. He gave Adam a side-glance before grabbing his phone and placing it in his drawer. He really didn't trust him. "I told you, I can't ask him again. I already mentioned Friday drinks at DuPont's. If I text him, I'll look pushy and/or pathetic."

"Or-r-r Rick will know it wasn't just a casual mention and it was an actual invitation to go *with you.*"

"Okay, but what if that's too much? What if he turns up, but he's not *that* interested in me, so he's decided to meet up with his friends, and while he's there, he'll just say a quick hello to me out of politeness?"

Adam smirked. "Is this how you act around Rick?"

"What do you mean?"

"All insecure and rambling sentences. 'Cause it's kind of cute."

"Shut up." His cheeks grew warm, but he ignored it and scowled at his friend.

"Anyway, it sure sounds like he's interested. One, he slung you over his shoulder and got intimate with your 'inner thigh.' Two, at the cabin, he kissed you. Three, that Dom-ish move in the truck when he gripped both your wrists sounds fuckin' smokin—"

"Adam!"

"What? You like him, and it sure seems like he likes you, so you need to stop stressing about Friday."

"But what if Rick doesn't come?"

Adam snickered. "I'd be happy to join you and 'help' him alo—"

"Shut up, idiot!" He punched Adam in the arm. "I'm serious. If Rick doesn't *attend* the wine bar on Friday, I have no idea what to do next. I totally blew it."

Adam snickered again.

"Adam! Get your mind out of the sewer for two seconds and help me."

"Okay, okay." Adam leaned against Luc's desk and stared out the window at the office parking lot. "Look, I know you said you acted like a bit of a fool on the trip, but surely Rick won't hold it against you? You said he was patient and—Hell, he even carried you home."

Luc groaned and put his head in his hands. "Ugh. Every time I think about it. Slung over his shoulder like a sack of...something with the blood rushing to my head as he—"

"I bet your blood rushed somewhere else too."

Luc gave Adam the evil eye. Sometimes his friend acted like an annoying, horny teenager.

Adam grinned. "Anyway, I bet it's not as bad as you think. A big, strong man like Rick probably gets off on slinging boys over his shoulder and taking them back to his cave—I mean—cabin."

"I am not a boy." Luc kept his expression stern, but flutters ran through his stomach. *Rick's boy.* It had a certain—no! He squirmed in his office chair. *No, don't let your imagination go there again.*

"Earth to Luc." Adam snapped his fingers in front of Luc's face.

"Huh?"

"You drifted off somewhere." Adam raised an eyebrow. "Was it the usual lumberjack daydream or a caveman scene this time?"

Heat rushed up Luc's neck and over his cheeks. *Damn it all to hell!* He should never have confided in Adam. A year ago, when Rick had merely been an impossible dream, telling Adam about his crush had seemed like a good idea, but right now, he regretted ever mentioning it. "If you don't stop, you are seriously jeopardizing our friendship."

Adam's smirk disappeared, and he rested his hand on Luc's shoulder. "Hey, I'm really sorry. I guess I'm teasing because I'm jealous. I mean, you might actually have a chance with Rick Masters! How amazing is that?"

"Well, I'll have to make a better impression than I have so far, and for that I need Rick to come to the wine bar and then..."

"And then?"

"Shit, I don't know. I really have no clue." What could he possibly do to impress Rick? Dress well, discuss wine, and be witty and charming? After the fiasco at the cabin, he would be happy to remain upright and not drool. Or bleed. "I need to—"

"Hey! There he is." Adam pointed toward the window and the parking lot beyond.

Luc's stomach muscles clenched as Rick's truck pulled into a parking space reserved for surveyors. He gulped as the big man slammed the truck door and strode toward the building. Despite their elevated position on the first floor, Rick could catch them staring.

But it didn't stop him ogling.

Hiking boots, faded jeans, and a tight, muscle-hugging black T-shirt. Sexy, close-cropped beard, unruly brown hair, and a confident stride. *Man, oh man.*

"Fuuck!" Adam leaned across the desk to follow Rick's progress as he neared the building, sighing as Rick disappeared from sight. "I totally get it. He is one hot piece of Muscle Bear!"

"Shh." Luc glanced at his partially open office door. "Keep your voice down."

Adam grinned. "Sorry. Again. But I really *do* get it. He is *fine* and *all* man." Adam stared vacantly out the window and whispered, "He makes you feel all tingly and breathless when he takes control and pounds you into the mattress."

"Wha-what? What the hell?" Bile rose in Luc's throat, and his heart rate hit overdrive. What was Adam saying? Had Adam had sex with Rick? Oh, God, he felt sick. He swallowed. Hard. "Ha-have you and Rick...? Please tell me you and Rick haven't..."

Adam whipped his head around to face Luc. "No! No, sorry. I meant guys *like* Rick—beefy and domineering. I would never do that to you."

Luc released the breath he had been unconsciously holding. "Okay. Okay, good." As his heart rate returned to normal, he shook his head. "Geez, Adam, first, could you keep those types of thoughts to yourself, and second, 'beefy and domineering'? Stereotyping much?"

Adam's attention returned to the view outside the window. "Yeah, I...guess...I should...n't..."

Luc frowned. "What are you looking at?" He leaned closer to the glass, scanning the grassy area and parking lot until he spied what had caught Adam's undivided attention. At the open door of a green truck, a man in black jeans stood bent over, his head and upper body hidden within the truck. He appeared to be searching for something. Luc bit his lip and grinned. "Nice ass."

Adam jumped. "Ah, yeah, I guess."

The man stood up, revealing a "beefy" enough frame to rival Rick's. He held a small blue book—a surveyor's field book. After slamming the truck door, the man strode toward the building and out of sight.

Luc studied his friend. "Hey, isn't that the surveyor, Jack—?"

"Jack Dawson. Yeah." Adam shoved his hands in his pockets and rocked on his heels. "So, anyway, umm...so, back to the Rick problem. Why don't we wait and see if he turns up at the bar on Friday? If he doesn't, well, we'll deal with it later, but if he does show up..." A slow smile spread across Adam's face.

"What?" Luc's stomach flip-flopped as Adam's smile widened into something to fear. "What evil plan are you hatching? I want your help, but I don't know if—"

"Relax. It's not evil. It's just a plan. A plan to 'hammer and peg' Rick. Get it? Hammer and peg, because you know...surveyor."

Luc raised an eyebrow and silently stared at Adam.

Adam raised his hands in the sign of surrender. "Someone left their sense of humor in the forest." He stalked to the door before twisting and speaking over his shoulder. "But never fear, I'll help you locate it, lock down its coordinates, and record them in a field book. Oh, and I'll help you get Rick too."

Shaking his head, Luc groaned at Adam's terrible, truly horrible jokes and waved his friend away. "Go. Now." He made a shooing gesture.

After Adam's grinning departure, Luc slumped into his chair. Stupid jokes aside, he appreciated Adam's offer of help, but wished Adam had shared his intentions. To date, he had made such a pathetic impression on Rick that he definitely needed all the assistance he could get.

*But what have I agreed to?*

# Chapter Nine

RICK DREW IN a deep breath and pushed open the door. DuPont's Wine Bar was exactly as he imagined. Stylish, sophisticated, and pretentious. He hated places like this. They transformed him into an overgrown, uncivilized oaf. Too many posh people for him to accidentally jostle, too many unpronounceable wines that tasted like vinegar, and a truckload of delicate, breakable wineglasses.

He tugged at the collar of his pale-blue business shirt—his only business shirt—and scanned the room for a familiar face. No sense lying to himself; he was searching for Luc. No matter how many times he resolved to ignore his attraction to Luc or reminded himself of the chasm between their lifestyles, he couldn't get the man out of his head. It had been four days since he had last seen Luc. Working at the reserve site had been interesting with definite moments of sexual tension. Which was why, for the first time, Rick had come to the wine bar. Against his better judgment.

In a booth at the back of the bar, Jack and Tony, two of his fellow surveyors, raised their hands in greeting. With a nod, he wove his way through the obstacle course of tables to his friends and slid into the horseshoe-shaped booth.

Tony slapped him on the back. "Rick, my man, glad you could make it. It's only taken you two years to accept our offer of a friendly Friday drink."

Jack shook his head. "Leave him alone, Tony. Rick, good to see you."

Rick pulled at his shirt collar. "You too, thanks."

Jack grabbed the pitcher of beer from the middle of the table and filled an empty glass. "Here you go."

Rick accepted the beer and raised an eyebrow. "They serve beer here?"

Jack snorted. "Yeah, there are enough of us schlebs here on a Friday to make beer profitable." He pointed to the second, empty pitcher. "As you can see, Tony does his best to make sure they don't change their minds."

"Hey! You drank half, and besides, we're both doing our bit to make sure the hoi polloi over there don't forget that real people work at the company too." He gestured rudely toward the group of people seated at a large table.

Jack frowned. "Seriously, you're not making any sense, and what on earth is a hoi polloi?"

Rick turned to the group Tony had indicated. And there was Luc, looking very different from the last time he had seen him. With his white collared shirt, perfectly groomed blond hair, a sexy red tie, and surrounded by office coworkers, Luc appeared the consummate businessman.

The blond guy seated beside Luc leaned in close and whispered in Luc's ear. The blood rushed through Rick's ears. *Damn it, who was that?* His grip on the beer glass tightened as Luc tipped back his head and laughed. Did Luc have a boyfriend? He could have sworn he didn't. During their time together, Luc had given him all kinds of signals, and "I have a boyfriend" wasn't one of them.

Jack's glass hit the table a little too hard. "Tony, they're not all bad. If you could stop judging them all for what they do and how they dress, you might find you like some of them."

Tony smirked. "Who is she?"

"What?"

"Who's the office girl you've got the hots for?"

Jack scowled. "Shut up, Tony."

Rick stared intently at his cardboard coaster as he shredded it into pieces. "Luc's okay."

"Luc?"

"Luc who?"

He swallowed. "Luc Weston. Cartographer. He came with me on some surveys. On one of them, we stayed at the cabin off Highway 70 for a couple of nights."

"Ha! I know exactly who you mean." Tony chuckled. "How did you get roped into babysitting the boss's nephew?"

"No, nothing like that. It's the job-swap program."

"Oh, not that crap," said Tony.

"Yeah, it's pretty stupid, but Luc was... At the beginning of the trip he was a bit of a jerk, but by the end he was...okay."

Tony nodded. "They're like animals."

"What?"

"Pardon?"

Tony grinned and then chugged the remainder of his beer before answering. "What I mean is that in their own habitat, surrounded by the same species, they act a certain way. It's expected of them. But when you take them away from the herd and out of their comfort zone, you get to see the real animal—or person."

Jack spluttered into his beer. "Ah, I think you've been watching too much of that nature channel stuff." He scanned the crowded bar. "So, is this Luc person here tonight?"

Rick nodded. "Yes. Northwest corner, white shirt and red tie."

"Yeah, okay," said Jack. "I've seen him around, but I hadn't realized he was the boss's nephew."

Tony gestured with his half-full beer glass. "Well, it looks like Luc's got his boyfriend with him."

Rick frowned as the sleazebag in the blue shirt ran his hand down Luc's arm. "Really? Is that his boyfriend?"

"Nah, I don't know. Just looks like that dude is all over him. Luc's got a sweet ride."

Rick choked on a mouthful of beer. "What the hell?"

Tony appeared confused. "What? He has. It's a fancy European thing. Like a Mercedes or a BMW or something."

Rick shook his head as he wiped his mouth with a napkin.

"Tony, you are a unique individual," said Jack.

"Thanks." Tony gulped his beer and then wiped his mouth on his sleeve. "So I heard from a friend, via a cute blonde in the aerial photography section, that Luc's gay? Hey!" He jerked upright. "Rick, you're gay!"

Rick chuckled. "Yes, Tony. You've known that for two years."

"Yeah, but if Luc's gay, and you're gay, and you just spent a couple of nights in a cabin together, you two must have... You know?

Jack smacked Tony in the back of the head. "Shut up, idiot. You're embarrassing yourself with your ignorance."

"What?" Tony scowled and rubbed his head. "If I was holed up in a cozy cabin with a hottie, I would."

Rick groaned. "No, we didn't, and it's not a forgone conclusion. It takes *two* willing participants."

Tony frowned as he tried to decipher Rick's reply.

Jack sighed. "Ignore him. He was dropped on his head when he was a baby."

"Hey! I was not."

The good-natured banter continued between Tony and Jack. Rick tried to listen, but his focus kept straying to Luc. And the sleaze ball who couldn't keep his hands to himself.

Surely, that couldn't be Luc's boyfriend. No way. He was too slick. Rick drew in a deep breath. Okay, now who had resorted to judging people by their appearance? And why should he care if Luc had a boyfriend? Despite the attraction, he doubted anything significant could develop between him and Luc. They were just too different. He released the mangled coaster and tried to be objective about the man now draped over Luc and whispering in his ear.

The blond guy was slim, clean-shaven, and good-looking in a sleek, office kind of way. Wearing the prerequisite business shirt (probably designer) and a bright-blue tie (assuredly silk), the guy had that arrogant, "I know I'm hot" look. So, after some objective consideration—*the guy's a slimy dickhead!*

He managed to grunt a few times in response to Jack and Tony's banter, but the scenario, and the dickhead on the other side of the room, held his attention like a...like a...like an animal stalking the enemy. Or dinner.

Rick's heart rate rose at each touch until he could no longer contain himself. "Who is that guy with Luc?"

Jack's brows drew down as he stared into his beer glass. "Adam Anderson."

"Ah, I've heard that name before. What's his story?"

Jack shrugged and pushed to his feet. "Who's for more beer?"

"You bet," said Tony.

Rick nodded absently, before sliding his gaze back to Luc. God, forget the other guy; Luc's smile sent electrified sparks shooting southward—straight to his cock. He wanted to kiss Luc again—taste those soft, luscious lips.

At the cabin, he had restrained himself. Too many thoughts and self-doubts swirling through his mind. Too many obstacles to give him pause. Like Luc's very wealthy uncle who also happened to be the man to sign his paycheck. And their obvious incompatibility—on so many different levels. Like his love of the outdoors, and Luc being an exact opposite. Rick had plans for the future that didn't include a city boy like Luc. But now, with someone else touching Luc....

*I want to be the only man with the right to touch him.*

Damn. He gulped down a mouthful of beer. Where had that idea come from? No man had ever made him territorial. The feeling was new and intense. He wanted to rip the interloper away, throw Luc over his shoulder again, take him back to his...home, and bury himself in Luc's fine ass. He wanted Luc's lips on his mouth. He wanted them wrapped around his—

"Here you go, one pitcher of beer for the real man's table."

"Yeeaah!" yelled Tony.

The loud yell cut through the buzz of conversation, garnering everyone's attention—including Luc's. Luc stared straight at him.

Rick's breaths grew shallow. Releasing his death grip on the glass, he began to raise his hand in greeting.

Adam Anderson—the prick—grabbed Luc's red tie and yanked him off-balance.

*What an asshole!*

He repeated the sentiment like a chant as Asshole Anderson touched and stroked and petted before unknotting Luc's tie and flicking open the shirt's top two buttons.

*Sleazy asshole! Fucking sexy red tie!*

His glass hit the table with a crash. "Damn, it's hot in here."

"What?"

"Shit, Rick. Give us both heart attacks why don't you?"

"Sorry, sorry, guys." He watched as Luc laughed, stood up, and headed for the corridor with the restrooms sign.

Rick slid out of the booth. "I need to take a leak."

"Okay."

"Sure, man."

With a sharp tug on his shirt collar, he strode after Luc. *Uncles and incompatibility be damned.*

# Chapter Ten

LUC AMBLED DOWN the dim corridor toward the men's room. With a yank on the end of his loose tie, the silk material slid from his neck. He was annoyed and a teeny bit dejected. Rick had arrived at the wine bar in all his huge glory, but the big man had ignored him. He could have visited Luc's table to say hi, or if he hadn't seen him until seated, at least acknowledged him in some way. Would a hand gesture, a quick wave from across the room, have killed him? Now Luc didn't know what to think or do. *Is Rick biding his time, or is he avoiding me?*

Despite the business shirt, or possibly because of it, Rick appeared totally out of place. With the white cotton stretched taut over hard muscles, the shirt appeared in danger of splitting at the seams and revealing the smooth, tanned curves of skin.

*I wish.*

Add in the faded-blue, ass-hugging jeans, and the man was totally delicious, delectable, edible, and lickable.

He sighed. *I wish.*

On the upside, Adam's flirting had taken his mind off Rick. It meant nothing and was obviously part of Adam's plan to make Rick jealous, but with Rick pointedly ignoring him for over an hour, the attention proved a balm to his ego. He wasn't going to let Rick's disinterest spoil his night. Much. Who needed attention from a big, sexy stud when you could have your purely platonic friend draped over you and whispering in your ear? With a wry grin, he spun the red tie and strolled down the hallway.

Mid-swing, a hand grabbed his red tie and jerked him off-balance, while another hand clamped around his bicep and spun him around. "Hey!" A solid wall of muscle blocked the corridor's dim light. "What the hell, man?" His head tipped back as his gaze roved over chest, neck, and beard. "Rick?"

Rick released his hold on Luc's arm and shifted from one foot to the other. "Yes. So, hi."

"Um, okay." He rubbed his arm. Rick's grip hadn't hurt, but the imprint of his hand tingled against his flesh. "Hi, to you too."

Rick's focus flicked to Luc's arm, and he frowned. "Sorry. I didn't mean to—"

"No, it's okay. You didn't." He dropped his hand to his side. No need to act like a wuss, as if he couldn't take a little arm gripping. Because he could. For sure. He'd be totally into that if Rick wanted to— *Shit, focus on the conversation.*

"Okay. Good. So, I made it here."

"So I see."

Rick's frown deepened into a scowl. "Were you intending to talk to me?"

"Well..." He could ask Rick the same question, but he looked a bit fierce, and there was no need to poke the bear. "I guess you looked pretty cozy with your friends. I wasn't sure if you wanted me to come over."

The muscles in Rick's jaw tensed. "Speaking of cozy, is that your boyfriend?"

"What? Who?"

"Anderson. Is Anderson your boyfriend?"

"No. I mean he's good-looking and funny, but I—" His heart raced as brown eyes narrowed. He swallowed. "No. He—he's just a friend."

Rick's shoulders lowered, and his expression turned neutral. Unreadable. "Okay. Good."

"Good?"

"Yeah, I wouldn't want to step on anyone's toes."

"Oh?" His heart rate increased. "So, were you thinking you might do something—with me—that could be toe-injury worthy?"

A smile curved across Rick's face as he leaned closer. "It's a possibility."

"Um. Okay." Breathe in. Breathe out. *Act cool. Act cool, but shit yeah!* "So, what did you have in mind?"

Rick glanced down the hallway toward the bar, before focusing on Luc again. "Well, I'd like to see you again, but somewhere else. Maybe dinner?"

"Um. Sure." *Yes!* Dinner at a nice restaurant with Rick would give him a chance to correct the bumbling fool impression. "How about Agostino's?"

Rick shook his head. "I was thinking more along the lines of Ben's Burgers."

Luc grimaced. Ben's Burgers wasn't quite what he had in mind. "What about Schapele's?"

"Okay, let's compromise. Dalton's." Rick moved closer, encroaching into his personal space and lowering the tone of his voice. "Dinner at Dalton's. With me."

Luc's breath caught. *Fuck me!* There was something about Rick's growly tone that sent sharp tingles zapping through his balls. "O-okay." Dalton's wasn't fancy, but it definitely ranked in a different class to a burger joint. Not that there was anything wrong with Ben's Burgers; they made fantastic food. But it was difficult to impress a guy with ketchup running down your hands and face.

"Tomorrow."

"Y-yes." His heart pounded in response to that one word. Those three syllables combined with Rick's intense stare were enough to have him agreeing to anything Rick wanted. Or commanded.

"Seven."

"Yes, Sir!" Heat crept up his neck and over his cheeks. "I mean, um." *Shit. I can't believe I just said "Sir."* He cleared his throat. "I-I mean, tomorrow at seven o'clock will be fine, Rick."

Rick grinned, before leaning so close his lips grazed Luc's ear. "Either form of address is acceptable, but I know which one I prefer."

Luc's knees went weak. The warm breath against his ear, and that hard body crowding him against the wall were enough to make him fall to his knees and lick Rick's hiking boots.

But that would be weird, so... No.

Ha! So much for his plan to impress Rick with his city polish, competence, and sophistication.

Rick growled against Luc's ear. "Do you know what I want to do right now?"

"N-no." Oh, God, he was turning into that babbling fool again. His knees shook as Rick's large paw—hand! Rick's hand cupped his jaw. "No! What?" *Oh, great, now I'm squawking.*

"This."

"Ahh!" As Rick bit his earlobe, a shudder raced through his body and his knees gave way. *Holy mother of...* He grabbed hold of Rick's waist to stop his descent to the ground and into total humiliation. A strong hand grasped his hip and steadied him, before sliding downward over his ass and gripping. Hard. *Oh, hell yeah.* His head swam and he swayed. Probably due to every drop of blood rushing to his dick. Did Rick intend to ravish him right there, in the middle of the hallway?

*Oh, God. A guy can hope.*

Rick pressed his nose to Luc's hair and inhaled deeply. "You smell good. Like—"

Loud laughter from the end of the corridor made Luc jump, and he pulled away from Rick's hold and stepped back a pace. "I, um." Shoving his hands into his pockets to conceal the evidence of his rock-hard erection, he smiled and nodded to the two women as they passed on their way to the bathroom. "So." He bit his lip and willed his dick to deflate. He needed to remember they were in a public place. Although it didn't seem to bother Rick.

Without any discernable expression, Rick stared at Luc. "So. Tomorrow then."

Luc nodded. Being bitten—*bitten*—by Rick was so damn hot he wasn't sure he could speak without babbling or squawking again. The man sure played havoc with his self-control. He cleared his throat. "I-I'll see you tomorrow."

"I'm looking forward to it."

"Yeah. Me too." With his hands still in his pockets, he rocked on his heels.

Rick's gaze flicked to his groin, and one corner of his mouth turned upward. "Tomorrow. Seven." With a wink, Rick turned and strode away.

His attention remained fixed on Rick's back (and ass) until he reached the end of the corridor and disappeared back into the bar.

*Shit.* The breath left his lungs in a loud rush. *Roll on tomorrow night.*

# Chapter Eleven

*WHAT WAS I thinking?*

Rick ceased drumming his fingers on the wooden tabletop to glance at his watch. Again.

6:57 p.m.

Asking Luc on a date must surely prove his insanity. *Pure lust scrambling my brain.*

On one hand, he truly believed this couldn't lead to anything lasting. They were too different. While he *loved* the outdoors, he had seen firsthand Luc's aversion to nature. His future plans didn't involve another person, let alone one with different values. As soon as possible, he intended to move from his basic two-bedroom apartment and live far from the city on his very own bought-and-paid-for plot of land just outside the White River National Park.

Secondly, Luc's uncle was in-your-face wealthy, owning one of the largest surveying and cartographic companies in the country with contracts for the government and private clients worth millions. Rick couldn't care less about the money, but he wouldn't fit in that world. Stereotyping? Probably. But the uncomfortable truth was that Luc's uncle could fire him if he didn't like him fraternizing with his nephew.

*But on the other hand, I can't stop thinking about him.*

*Maybe I should just enjoy it—whatever it is—while it lasts?*

He scanned the restaurant. Saturday night at Dalton's was busy. In the spirit of compromise, he had settled on this place because it wasn't too fancy. Not like Luc's other suggestions. Agostino's? Seriously? No way would he ever fit in at a place like Agostino's. And Schapele's wasn't much different. But Dalton's sturdy, if slightly small booths, relaxed atmosphere, and casual dress code placed it just inside his comfort zone. With his black T-shirt, best jeans, and newly trimmed beard, he didn't stand out in the crowd. He shifted in his seat, rearranging his legs to fit more comfortably.

7:01 p.m.

Movement at the restaurant door caught his attention, and his breath caught.

Luc.

Dressed in a black leather jacket that probably cost more than the entire contents of Rick's closet and jeans that clung in all the very finest places, Luc followed the waiter's gesture and headed in his direction. As he tracked Luc's progress across the restaurant, all his logical thoughts of incompatibility and caution were stomped on and smothered by pure lust.

*Damn.*

Luc arrived and smiled. "Hi."

*Oh, shit!* He shifted in his seat to ease the pressure in his jeans. "Hi."

As Luc lowered himself into the opposite side of the booth, his knee nudged the inside of Rick's thigh. "Sorry."

"S'okay." The vision of his splayed thighs beneath the table, bracketing Luc's legs, flashed through his mind. Would they touch each time one of them moved? His very long legs often got in the way, especially in booths, but he wasn't usually so hyperaware of respective leg positions. As Luc settled into his seat, both their legs knocked together again—Luc's knees against the inside of Rick's thighs. Both thighs. Luc's startled stare caught his before a faint flush crept up his neck. He had obviously realized...and was probably picturing the splayed leg scenario beneath the table.

*If he only knew what my dick was doing.*

Luc bit his lip and picked up a menu. "S-so." He cleared his throat. "What's good here?"

"Well, what do you like? Vegetarian? Chicken? Meat?" He pulled his legs in, nudging Luc's knees again.

The flush on Luc's neck deepened and spread upward over his cheeks, but he didn't move away from the contact.

He smiled and Luc smiled back. "Everything is decent, but the burgers are especially good."

Luc gave a short laugh. "No, no burgers."

He raised an eyebrow. "Not a burger kind of guy?"

"Sure, but not on a first date. I like to show off my dexterous use of cutlery and refined table manners."

"So you prefer places like Agostino's and Schapele's?" His smile disappeared.

"What? No!" Luc bit his lip. "I like all kinds of restaurants. I even love Ben's Burgers. It's just, I mean, it's hard to impress when you're chowing down on a delicious but sloppy mess."

"Mmm." He watched Luc fidget for a bit before deciding to let him off the hook. "I see your point. Burgers are probably a third-date outing." His stomach gave a flip as Luc grinned and bit his lip, drawing his attention to its plumpness. He wanted to bite that lip, and then suck it into his mouth and soothe the hurt. Then bite some more. He shifted in his seat and willed himself to stop thinking about all the other places he could bite Luc.

*Civilized. Keep it civilized.*

The waiter arrived, giving Rick a few seconds to calm down and a chance to study Luc. He had to smile at Luc's serious expression as he quizzed the attentive waiter over the ingredients of various meals. Did this one have garlic in the dressing? Was that one grilled or fried? Could he have that particular dish without the ginger?

In Rick's world, food was fuel. When hungry, he ate, and he wasn't fussy. His food decisions were a tad basic. Meat, chicken, or fish. With vegetables, rice, or pasta. Spices were fine, but he didn't care which ones. He would eat just about anything.

As the waiter departed, Luc began toying with his cutlery. "So...here we are."

"Yes." Rick's jeans grew tight as he focused on the telltale signs of Luc's nervousness. A faint flush across his cheekbones, lip biting, and avoiding eye contact. He couldn't work out why Luc's reactions were all so damn appealing. Was Luc currently jumping and jiggling his leg beneath the table? One way to find out. He moved one of his splayed legs inward until he made contact with the denim-clad jackhammer. For a few seconds, the friction sent vibrations up his leg to his—

Luc's leg froze, and his startled stare locked on Rick. "Sorry."

"It's okay." With a mental groan, he eased his leg away from temptation. Not the time or place. "So, tell me what you like."

"Like?"

"To do. For fun. Entertainment."

"Oh, well, I like going out to eat. Lunch, dinner, coffee, and cake. Movies, especially action and superhero, but I'll watch anything. Except horror. I hate horror. And chainsaw massacres. Do you like horror?"

"No, I—"

"Antiquing."

"Pardon?"

"I love antiquing, rummaging around in stores jam-packed full of old and interesting stuff. Of course I never buy any of it because my apartment is modern and it wouldn't suit."

"So why…?"

"It's fun."

Rick raised an eyebrow. He was never one for pointless action.

"What? Haven't you ever window-shopped just for the hell of it?"

"I don't believe so. No."

"Well, maybe you should try it sometime."

"Mmm. Maybe."

"And baseball."

"Ah, I have tried baseball."

"No, I meant I like going to baseball games. For fun. But not football. Who wants to freeze their ass and fingers off in the middle of winter?"

As the discussion turned to the weather and then their recent surveying trips, Luc visibly relaxed, and his nervous energy calmed. Rick couldn't take his eyes off his gorgeous dinner partner as Luc laughed in that self-deprecating way, reminiscing about his mountain mishaps and the rabid killer squirrel.

He liked Luc's smile.

Among other things.

Did it really matter if they had different interests? Luc liked fancy restaurants and had a slight problem with the outdoors. So what? They were both reasonable human beings capable of compromise, and Luc had proved to be a good sport about it. They weren't contemplating marriage or anything. And so what if Luc's uncle—Rick's boss—decided to object to them fraternizing in a more than Friday-night-drink-with-your-colleagues way? He didn't need *this* job in particular. His qualifications and experience could land him a job in any of ten to fifteen companies—if the need arose.

Nope. Watching Luc's animated smile as they finished their coffee, he decided to ignore all thoughts of caution and enjoy.

His dick agreed.

# Chapter Twelve

LUC'S BREATH CAUGHT as a gust of cold night air slapped him in the face. The chill shocked his system after the warmth of the restaurant, and he scrambled to put his leather jacket back on. Conscious of Rick watching, he shrugged into the jacket. "Okay. Done."

"Not quite." Rick reached out and tugged at the neckline, settling the collar into the correct position and smoothing the leather, his hand lingering on Luc's shoulder. "There."

"Thanks." He dropped his focus to Rick's chest. *What now?* "So, umm, my car is..."

"Where did you park?"

He shivered as Rick removed his hand and stepped back, missing the brief contact. "In the lot near the hardware store."

"I'll walk with you."

"Are you...?" Had Rick also parked his truck there, or did he want to "walk" Luc to his car? Should he ask? Did it matter? "Umm, okay."

They headed south along the sidewalk, side by side, but never touching. Silent. Luc's nerves began to kick in. Should he make small talk? Despite the easy conversation in the restaurant, Rick was usually a man of few words. Maybe Rick liked the silence.

The noise and lights from the businesses lining the main street receded as they turned onto the side street. The streetlights seemed dimmer and the shadows deeper.

Normally, when on his own, he would stay alert and walk faster. After a side-glance at Rick, he relaxed. No doubt, the hulking form of the man beside him would make any would-be assailants think twice.

He looked down as warmth engulfed his icy hand.

"God, you're freezing." Rick raised their clasped hands. "Is this okay?"

A quick scan of the street confirmed what he already knew. Deserted. "Umm, yeah. Sure."

As he strolled along the street beside Rick, one hand encased in delicious warmth and the other shoved in his pocket, a sense of calm stole through him.

*Rick will look after me.*

*What the—?* Okay, calmness destroyed. Where the hell had that stupid thought come from? He wasn't some delicate wuss who needed someone to keep him safe. He had managed exceedingly well on his own so far. Thank you very much.

"Hey." Rick squeezed his hand. "You okay?"

"Huh?"

"You seem tense."

"Oh." He forced his muscles to relax and eased his grip on Rick's hand. "No, I'm good. My car is over there. Behind that red pickup." He slowed his steps. "So, I guess I'll see you later."

Rick tugged on his hand and headed toward the car. "We're not there yet." He towed Luc around the pickup, only stopping when they reached the driver's door of his car. "The perfect parking place."

"What?" He frowned and scanned the unremarkable lot.

Rick raised their clasped hands to shoulder height and altered his hold, slowly slotting his fingers between Luc's before stepping forward, crowding him against the side of the car, face-to-face, their chests a whisper away from touching. "Dim light, quiet, camouflaged and hidden by the pickup; I'm glad you didn't park on the main street."

Luc tipped his head back and stared. "Wha—what?" His heart pounded, and his brain refused to compute Rick's words. The warmth emanating from Rick's body wrapped around him, blanketing him from the world.

Rick leaned down and murmured, "Now we can say good night properly."

Luc's heart went into overdrive, and he swallowed the large lump lodged in his throat. Rick meant kissing, right? He didn't want to misinterpret and make a fool of himself. Again. "I-I, ah I—"

"I'll rephrase that. I'm *going* to kiss you. Now."

Rick's free hand cupped his jaw, the rough skin radiating heat and warming his tense face. With the uncertainty gone, his mind cleared, and he melted into the big man's touch. "Please." He closed his eyes as Rick leaned closer. Beard bristles tickled his cheek. Breath whispered across his mouth. Lips touched, oh so softly. A soft sigh escaped his lips. He wanted more. "Please."

With a ragged groan, Rick disentangled their hands and slid his downward to cup Luc's ass. Surging forward, he aligned their bodies from chest to knee, trapping Luc between cold metal and his warm, hard body. Firm pressure beneath his jaw forced him to tip his head back. His lips parted, and Rick claimed them in a hot, hard kiss. *Oh. My. God.*

He grabbed onto Rick's shirt and held tight as sensations bombarded him. Ragged breaths. The scent of pine trees. Soft lips pressing hard, sliding, nibbling, devouring. Rick's tongue sweeping across his bottom lip, caressing, seeking, and then plunging inside. Quivers ran through his stomach, and his cock hardened.

Overwhelmed, he couldn't think—he didn't want to. He moaned as Rick thrust his rigid length against his hip, his huge body enveloping and overpowering him. Wrapped in Rick's arms, he couldn't move—he didn't need to. A shudder ran through him as Rick dug his fingers into his ass cheek and pulled him hard up against his groin—grinding. Luc's cock pulsed, and he moaned into Rick's demanding mouth.

Rick had total control over him.

And it felt so right.

His muscles relaxed, his body instinctively surrendering to the strength surrounding him. Fears faded, and the world outside Rick's arms became unimportant. Rick plundered his mouth, stamping his claim and stealing his breath with ball-tingling kisses. Luc's focus narrowed to lips and tongues.

Breathe in. Breathe out.

Hard cocks and hands.

Breathe in. Breathe out.

Strong arms and warmth and safety.

So very, very right.

"Damn." Rick eased his mouth away and dragged in harsh breaths. "So damn sexy. You make me want to…" He inhaled and exhaled slowly.

*What? I make him want to…what?* Luc was so turned on he would do anything Rick wanted. He would happily fall to his knees and suck Rick off.

*Or let him rip off my pants and take me right here, up against the car.*

Rick placed a lingering but light kiss to Luc's lips. "I believe it's time to say good night."

*No, no, no.* He groaned and pressed his aching cock against Rick's thigh.

Rick gave a firm squeeze to his ass cheek before releasing his hold and leaning back. Already missing the contact, Luc shivered as the chilly air curled around him. "I—ahh." Rick's thumb sliding across his lower lip halted his fractured thoughts and words.

"I need to see you again. Lunch. Monday."

"O-okay." He couldn't have formed a full sentence if he tried—even if Rick wasn't staring at his mouth and rubbing at his lip as if it fascinated him.

"Twelve o'clock?"

"Yeah."

"Good. I'll text you." Rick dropped his hand to his side and stepped back a pace.

"'Kay." Forcing his limbs to move, Luc dug his keys from his pocket and opened the car door. "So... Good night." He bit his lip and stood by the open door. With a foot of space between them, he shuffled his feet, awkward and unsure.

The edges of Rick's mouth curved upward in a slow smile, before he leaned in for a quick, hard kiss. "See you Monday. Drive safely."

"Okay. Monday." In an undignified scramble, he all but fell into the car and slammed the door closed. As he drove off, he couldn't stop smiling. The best date ever and another one to look forward to. He shifted in his seat to ease the pressure in his jeans.

But first, he had a date with a hot shower and his right hand.

# Chapter Thirteen

AS HE EXITED the office, Luc allowed his grin free rein. Like a man breaking out of his bindings, he burst onto the street and strode along the pavement. All morning he had suppressed his buoyant mood, wary of inviting remarks about getting lucky or laid. Of course, he hadn't been laid, but there had been spectacular, down-and-dirty kisses to rival any from his previous experiences.

Leaning—no, sprawling against the car with the hulking man plastered to his front from chest to knee was something he wouldn't forget. And hoped to experience again. Very soon. With his mouth and body, Rick had taken control. Dominated. Luc's balls tingled, and his stomach fluttered. Damn, just the thought of it. From mere kisses.

He laughed, ignoring the startled stares of passersby. There had been nothing *mere* about those kisses. They had satisfied him in a way, other than the obvious, that he couldn't exactly explain, but he'd bet money it had something to do with the way Rick manhandled him.

And then gently kissed and stroked to soothe.

Rough yet gentle, domineering yet caring—a heady combination. Wrapped in Rick's arms, he had been overwhelmed and powerless, yet totally safe. More than twice his size, Rick could easily hurt him, but while Rick's physical attributes could intimidate, his manner engendered trust. He probably shouldn't trust him after such a short time, but he did. And he couldn't wait to touch and taste Rick again, but for now, a friendly lunch together at a café would have to be enough.

With a hard shove, the glass café door opened. In his text, Rick had suggested the Niche Café, a nice place with raw-wood floors and dark-green vinyl booths lining the back wall. The remainder of the seating consisted of stylish, dark wooden chairs and tables. Only a short walk from the office, the café was close, but not too close, minimizing the odds of running into coworkers. Not that he worried too much; it would be easy enough to brush it aside as two employees meeting up for lunch.

He spied Rick at a booth in the back corner and made his way through the crowd. Rick must have arrived early to score the prime position. He drew in a calming breath. Okay, keep it low-key. No need to embarrass himself by acting like a besotted fool. With a shy smile, he slid into the booth beside Rick. "Hi." Flutters ran through his gut as one corner of Rick's mouth curled upward.

*Oh, man, I am so screwed.*

Rick slid his hand under the table and gave Luc's thigh a quick squeeze. "Hi, yourself."

"I-I, umm..." *Yep. So screwed.* He cleared his throat. "It's pretty busy today. I guess we should order now, or we'll be waiting all afternoon for our food."

"I already ordered for both of us. I figured you'd only have an hour for lunch, so I ordered a couple of different things. You can choose which one you like best, or we can share. Is that okay?"

"Sure." A happy glow filled his chest. Rick had thought about what was best—for him. Shit, now *that* was a sappy thought, definitely befitting a besotted fool. He should probably be annoyed by the loss of control, but he had begun to suspect this relationship dynamic could be what he needed. Of course, the thought wasn't totally new to him. He had done his fair share of Internet searching and stumbled across the whole submissive concept—and scared himself shitless in the process. Definitely too hard-core for him, but this thing with Rick was…

Big, beautiful Rick.

A shiver snaked through him as Rick's massive hand spanned the back of his head, and a possessive brown-eyed gaze swept over him. His heart raced as Rick drew him forward and claimed his mouth in a quick, hard kiss, leaving him breathless.

As he settled back into his seat, the warmth from Rick's hand lingered on the back of his head. The grin on his face surely appeared dopey, but at that moment, with the tingle of Rick's kiss still on his lips, he really didn't care.

The food arrived, and Luc made his choice based on mess-making potential. He might be willing to grin like a fool, but he wasn't quite ready to eat like a pig in front of Rick. A man had to have some standards!

"Food okay?"

He nodded. And grinned. *Fool!*

"Good."

At other tables, plates clattered and people talked and laughed, but Rick and Luc remained silent as they ate. With a couple of quick side-glances, he noted Rick's relaxed posture. The lack of words should have felt strange, but it didn't. Silence on a date made Luc nervous, and his usual response would be to make inane remarks about their surroundings or blurt out random thoughts, while trying to guess his date's mood. But Rick didn't appear worried by the lull in their conversation and seemed happy to focus on eating. With Rick, the silence felt comfortable and suspiciously like contentment. As if a constant flow of words would spoil the calm accord between them. Which was unexpected—in a good way, but still a little weird.

After another few minutes of eating, Rick swallowed a mouthful of soda and then smiled. "So, tell me, have you always worked with your uncle's company?"

"Yes. Since I was a kid."

Rick raised an eyebrow. "A kid?"

He nodded. "I've been hanging around his office since I was about six years old. That's when I went to live with him after my parents died. Car accident."

"Damn. I'm sorry." Beneath the table, Rick squeezed Luc's thigh.

"It's okay. It was a long time ago, and I was lucky to have Uncle J. Back then the company was half the size and located in an old building downtown." He smiled as the memories washed over him. "Uncle J would pick me up every day after school, and I'd wander about the office pestering people to let me draw maps. Uncle J finally gave me my own tilted drafting board and a set of drafting pens, and I became a 'junior draftsman.' I have the permanent ink to prove it."

"Permanent ink?"

He offered his forefinger for Rick's inspection. "Black ink spots."

Rick cradled Luc's left hand and inspected the side of his finger. "It's beneath the surface of your skin. Like a tattoo."

"The sign of a true draftsman, or so Uncle J says." A shiver crept up his spine as Rick ran his thumb over the small black marks. "The tips of those Rotring pens are sharp. I lost count of the times I stabbed myself—hence, the ink." Reluctantly, he pulled his hand away. "Of course, no one uses pens anymore; it's all computer-aided drafting now. Uncle J was one of the first to transition to CAD systems, and it paid off. As you know, the company is now one of the biggest in the country."

Rick nodded. "Do you think you'll keep working for him?"

"That's the plan. Uncle J's already told me that the company will be mine when he retires—mine to make or break." He smiled wryly. "But no pressure."

"That's a lot of responsibility."

"Yeah." His smile faded, and he stared at his empty plate, the weight of the future pressing on him and dampening his mood.

"Hey." Rick curled his hand around Luc's neck and massaged the tense muscles.

"Sorry." He sat up straighter and forced a smile. "So, any surveys with overnighters at the cabin planned?"

"Mmm, later in the week. Tony Rossi and I are both heading out that way, so we'll be sharing the cabin. Probably two nights." Rick released Luc's neck and slid his hand under the table, resting it high on Luc's thigh.

Luc swallowed. "I-I guess Tony will be a lot less trouble than I was."

Rick made eye contact, his expression smoldering. "I'd take you instead of Tony any time." Rick leaned closer, his breath whispering across Luc's cheek like a caress. "Any time."

"Mmm." A soft whimper escaped his lips as Rick claimed his mouth in a firm yet gentle kiss, sending his heart rate soaring.

*Holy mother of...!*

He loved Rick's kisses and the way they made him feel, but as he settled back into his seat, he couldn't suppress the surge of self-consciousness. With his heart still thumping, he scanned the other diners, looking for familiar faces. There didn't appear to be anyone from work in the café, and no one stared at them. He turned his attention back to Rick and took a gulp of his drink. The way the big man stared at him, bold and possessive, made his stomach quiver. He didn't yet know how to label what lay between them, and perhaps he shouldn't even try.

*But it sure feels good.*

# Chapter Fourteen

LUC HUNCHED HIS shoulders as the cold night air curled around him, poking and probing his leather jacket while searching for a way inside. He moved a little closer to Rick's side as they walked, hoping the big man's bulk would shield him from the chilled breeze. Wearing jeans and only a long-sleeved black shirt, Rick didn't appear bothered by the cold.

They were on their way to a jazz club—Rick's choice. Luc didn't know what to expect. He had never been one for the club scene, but he imagined a jazz club would be an altogether different experience. Of course, he'd heard live jazz before at the city's annual open-air festival, but never at a club.

"It's just down here." Rick pointed before settling his hand on the curve of Luc's back and guiding him down a narrow alley. A lone door glowed red under a neon sign. "Armstrong's." Simple and succinct.

"Huh."

"What?" Rick paused beside the entrance and pulled him closer.

"Is Armstrong the owner, or is it named after Louis?"

"Both."

He smiled as Rick held the door open for him and made sure to body brush him as he entered the club. Despite the public setting, he couldn't resist touching. Inside, the dim lighting and low hum of conversation intrigued him. Tiny round tables just large enough to hold a couple of drinks stood clustered on one side of the room. On the other, a scuffed parquet dance floor lay empty and waiting. On a small stage, at an old upright piano, a young man sat playing chords. Soft and slow. It brought to mind the old movies he used to watch as a child every Saturday afternoon. The only things missing were a thick smoky haze and the threat of raids.

A shiver ran down his spine as Rick spoke, bringing him back to the present. "An amazing trio plays here, but they must be taking a break. Let's find a table."

Luc settled onto the replica antique chair and held his breath as he waited to see if the flimsy structure would hold Rick's massive frame. From Rick's careful movements and expression, the big man most likely feared the same thing. The chair creaked ominously but stayed in one piece. With a silent sigh of relief, Luc gestured to the barely lit dance floor. "Do people dance here?"

"Yes."

"Have you ever?"

"Sure."

"So...you've brought female friends here?" Was it obvious he was fishing for details of Rick's dating past?

Rick smiled and shook his head. "No. No lady friends."

"But...you said you've danced."

"So, you're assuming I need a female for that?"

"Well, I... Yeah."

"This place welcomes everyone. A few years ago, a guy I dated suggested it. I like it because it's casual. No pretenses. No judgment. Just jazz."

Luc frowned. "I'm having trouble picturing you dancing. With anyone."

"Well, dancing could be overstating. I try not to move my feet and keep my elbows in. It's more like shuffling and swaying."

"Still..." He bit his lip and scanned the club and its patrons. Would Rick expect him to slow dance in front of all these people? His leg started jiggling of its own accord.

"Did you think I only did mountain-man stuff?"

"Sort of. Dancing just doesn't seem like the kind of thing you would do. I mean, look at you." He gestured toward Rick and all his bulky hotness.

Rick raised an eyebrow. "Is that another 'someone like you' comment?"

"What? No! Shit no. I-I have to explain about that. I swear I didn't mean it like that at all. I-I meant it in a positive way. 'Someone like you' as in hot, rugged, and having no use for a useless little cooler bag." His heart raced as he fidgeted with one of the cardboard coasters. "I mean, you probably chill your food in a cold river. Or the snow. Or—or not at all. I... Shit." His shoulders slumped. "You've seen my stupid mouth in action around you. I swear it's not connected to my brain."

Rick covered Luc's agitated hand with his and gave it a gentle squeeze. "It's okay. I believe you." He leaned in close until his arm pressed against Luc. "And I would like to see your mouth in action. *Around me.*"

Rick's stare sent shivers through him. *Oh, hell, yeah.* The man was so fucking sexy, and he'd bet his BMW they were both thinking about his mouth wrapped around Rick's cock. Sweat broke out under his arms. Why was his jacket so stifling all of a sudden? "Fuck, it's so hot." He started struggling to shuck the leather sauna from his shoulders.

"So damn hot." Rick grinned in that sexy way that seemed to say "You're so cute."

"Shit." His cock twitched and his face burned. When he had finally freed himself from the uncooperative garment, he dropped it in his lap. If Rick kept up his sexy teasing, he would need to conceal a certain something. Time to shift the conversation to safer topics. "So, um, you haven't ever said. W-were you born here?"

"Yes, I lived here until the age of five."

"And then?"

"My mother remarried. My stepfather didn't want to stay here, so we moved to New York."

"Oh, wow."

"And then Chicago, Philadelphia, Boston, and a few others in-between."

"Did you like living in those big cities?"

"No. I hated it. So did my mother. They were cramped and overcrowded—suffocating. We never stayed for more than a year or two in each one."

"That must have been tough as a kid. Difficult to make friends."

Rick nodded. "Yes. Very."

"I can't imagine moving so often—to never feel like you had a permanent home."

"I moved back here to go to college. My father still lived here, so it seemed the logical choice."

"What about your mother?"

"A few years later, she divorced and followed me. She has a nice house in the suburbs."

Movement on the stage caught their attention as an old man holding a saxophone stepped up to the microphone. "We're back. We're gonna start with some slow songs for the lovers here tonight. If anyone feels like dancin', y'all go right ahead."

The music began. Three men, a piano, saxophone, and bass playing mellow, sultry sounds that soothed his nerves. More than a few couples moved to the dance floor. Guys and their girls, and then two guys together. No one seemed to pay them any mind.

Rick held out his hand. "Dance with me."

"Umm." He turned to look around the room.

"No. Look at me." Rick cupped Luc's cheek and turned his head back toward him. "Dance with me."

Luc's heart began to pound, and he couldn't have looked away from the intense stare if he'd tried. "Okay," he whispered.

Clasping his hand, Rick rose and towed him to the far side of the dance floor. Pulled into the big man's embrace, Luc stood stiffly, unsure of how to act or feel. Shit. This was so far out of his comfort zone he didn't know if...

"Relax." Rick tucked Luc's face into his shoulder and ran his hand over his back in soothing strokes. "No one cares."

He snuck a glance at the other gay couple. They both seemed at ease, smiling lovers' secret smiles and talking quietly as they swayed to the music. Rick began to sway and shuffle—just as he said. Gradually, the smooth melody and Rick's warmth seeped into his senses, and he melted into strong arms.

"That's it." Rick nuzzled his hair and hummed in a deep, soft voice against his head. As Rick's hand slid to his waist and pulled him tightly against him, Luc's dick ached with the delicious pressure. Each sway brought friction and focus. The crowd evaporated, and Rick became the center of his world. One of those old-time raids could have happened around him, and he wouldn't care.

Time passed. He didn't know or care how much. For a few blissful minutes, or maybe hours, they embraced and moved together as one. The increasingly familiar and addictive scent of warm male with earthy undertones curled around him, tethering him to his man more securely than ropes.

*Although, ropes are an intriguing idea.*

With his eyes closed, he bit his lip and rubbed his face on Rick's shoulder. As the music wrapped around him, his senses sharpened, hyperfocusing on every detail of their bodies pressed together. Chest to chest. His shirt scraped across his nipples, each miniscule movement of the fabric catching on his flesh and causing little bites of pain. *So good.* He flattened his palms against the muscles of Rick's back. Rick's hands slid a fraction lower to rest at the base of his spine—a position just shy of acceptable in a public place. His dick strained against denim and pulsed with every slide and drag of jeans, thigh, and—*oh, fuck*—Rick's hard cock. He tightened his arms and pressed harder, moaning into Rick's neck as the rigid steel ground into him.

*Fuckfuckfuck. Who knew dancing could feel like this?*

Another song ended but slid effortlessly onto the next. With a slight nudge, Rick steered and shuffled him backward toward a shadowed alcove. Obscured from the other dancers, Rick cupped his cheek and dove in for a hot, wet kiss. Lips and tongues and mingled breaths, the big man kissed as if their mouths would never meet again. As if kisses were illegal and they risked everything in those few desperate moments.

*Oh, God, yes. Yes, yes, yes.*

Luc's knees wavered in their resolve to keep him upright. He needed skin and sweat and slickness. And a bed. Or a couch. Or the goddamn bare floor would do. He didn't care; he just needed Rick above him and inside him. Now.

With his dick aching and on the verge of exploding, he wrenched his lips away from Rick's mouth and dragged air into his lungs. "Rick. Can we—"

"Leave?"

"Yeah."

Rick stole another quick kiss and then snagged Luc's bottom lip between his teeth and growled. The vibrations traveled south, straight to his—

*Oh, shitshitshit.* Too close. He really didn't want to come in his pants.

With a gentle nip, Rick released his lip. "It is time to leave, but not for the reason you mean."

"Wha-what? Why?"

"I'm sorry. I have to travel to a survey site tomorrow, and I need to get up at 4:00 a.m."

"But we could still..."

"No." Rick rested his forehead against Luc's. "I should have left for the survey this afternoon, but I wanted to see you and bring you here. Damn. I didn't think this through. I so want to take you home and stay with you. God, how I want to stay. But I don't want to sneak away in the early hours. It wouldn't feel right."

"But it wouldn't be sneaking if I know it's going to happen." He stared at Rick and tried to *will* him to agree. He even gave a little nudge of his hips to remind Rick what was on offer.

Rick grinned and brushed his lips across Luc's hair. "Patience. It'll be worth it."

Yes, he was positive it would be, but... *Shit, the frustration might kill me first.*

# Chapter Fifteen

RICK GLANCED AT his passenger, assessing his denim shorts and tight black T-shirt. Luc's clothes would do nicely for the activity he had planned. It was Saturday afternoon, and he had just picked Luc up at his apartment. For days, he had been counting the hours until he could see Luc again. Dropping him off at his apartment after their night at the jazz club had been torture, and he'd almost wavered in his decision not to stay the night. But it would have only been a half night, and the early morning departure would have felt too much like the end of a hookup.

And Luc was no hookup. He deserved more.

Beside him, Luc repeatedly rubbed his palms over his thighs. "So, is my outfit all right?"

"Perfect."

"'Cause I wasn't sure. I mean, you said shorts, but nothing too tight, so I thought these were the best option."

Rick reached over and covered Luc's hand, stilling the nervous action and caressing Luc's bare thigh with his fingers. "They're perfect."

Luc started jiggling his other leg, his heel tapping against the floor of the truck. "Are you going to tell me where we're going?"

"No."

"A hint?"

"Nope."

"Is it far?"

Rick smiled. "If you stop the nervous jiggling, I might tell you."

Luc's leg ceased moving. "Sorry."

"It's okay." After giving Luc's fingers a quick squeeze, he returned his hand to the steering wheel. "There's no need to be worried. I wouldn't take you anywhere that I didn't think you could handle."

"That's...not very reassuring."

"Well, we're here, so the uncertainty is over."

After parking near a gray metal building resembling a large shed, he removed the keys and turned to Luc. "Ready?"

Luc frowned as he stared at the structure. "Is it a factory?"

"No. Come on; all will be revealed soon."

They exited the truck, and Rick led the way to the entrance. He was sure Luc would read the business name printed on the glass door and balk at entering, but he entered without comment or reaction.

Until he viewed the interior and froze on the spot.

"Rock climbing?"

If highness of voice was a fear indicator, then Luc currently bordered on freaking-the-hell-out.

Rick curled his hand around the back of Luc's neck and rubbed his thumb through the short hairs at the base of his skull. "Yes. Indoor rock climbing in a controlled environment with experienced staff to assist." He leaned in close, his lips brushing the top of Luc's ear. "It's going to be fine. Just breathe and trust me to look after you."

The breath Luc had been holding rushed out, before he leaned into Rick's hold. "Ha-have you done this before?"

"Yes. Here, and in various national parks."

Luc raised his head and stared into Rick's eyes. "I've never done anything like this. I mean, you've seen me trying to walk along a dirt trail. This is..."

He stroked the back of Luc's neck in firm, soothing circles. "I know, but I'll take care of you. You just need to follow my instructions and everything will be okay."

Luc's tense shoulders lowered as he expelled another breath. "Okay. Okay, I trust you."

"Thank you." Smiling, he pressed a quick kiss to Luc's temple. "Now let's go hire some gear and have some fun."

Striding toward the counter, his hand still cupping Luc's neck, he ignored the small scoff of disbelief Luc made. Luc probably viewed this as anything but fun, an ordeal to suffer through, but Rick was determined to change his mind. He would take care of Luc, ease his fears, and show him they could enjoy something clearly out of Luc's comfort zone.

In quick order, he paid the fee, collected the harnesses and climbing shoes, and steered Luc to an area with low bench seats and a row of blue lockers. "We can stow our shoes and belongings in the locker. Make sure your pockets are empty. We don't want to cause a riot by showering people below with cash." He grinned at Luc's startled expression. "Or credit cards."

One corner of Luc's mouth began to curve upward, before he halted it by biting his lip.

Rick breathed a silent sigh of relief at the slight sign of Luc's nervousness lessening. He wanted Luc to not only succeed and gain a sense of accomplishment, but also enjoy the experience, and hopefully, be open to a repeat performance. Perhaps one day they could progress to climbing on some easy rock faces in a nearby national park.

*Wow, getting ahead much?*

He glanced at Luc's face, noting the tense expression had returned.

*Okay. One step at a time.*

He toed one of his shoes off and then stood watching as Luc sat down and began fumbling his shoelaces with trembling fingers.

"Fuck. I'm so nervous I can't even get my shoes off. Talk about pathetic."

"Hey." He knelt down and placed his hand on Luc's knee. "Don't say that. Being nervous about something you've never done is natural. Don't be so hard on yourself. Okay?"

Luc stared at him for a second before dropping his gaze to the floor. "Okay."

He gave Luc's knee a quick squeeze and stood up. "Take your time. There's no rush."

After drawing in and then releasing a deep breath, Luc untied his laces and gave Rick a quick smile. Reassured by Luc's actions, Rick continued his own preparations while keeping an eye on Luc in case he showed signs of panicking or needing help.

With their belongings stowed and their climbing shoes on, he guided Luc to the base of the climbing wall. Not wanting Luc to become overwhelmed by the sheer size of the wall and what they were about to do, he explained each of his actions while fastening Luc's harness. Hoping to convey confidence and a sense of calm, he spoke clearly and kept his tone low.

Luc stood, glaze-eyed and wooden as if he had checked out of his body.

With a tug on Luc's harness, Rick towed him toward one of the ropes suspended from the top of the wall. "I'm going to fasten this to your harness. This belay will—"

"Stop!" Luc repeatedly dragged air into his lungs. "I-I know this will sound stupid, but c-could you stop telling me details about the equipment? Just tell me what I have to do."

"Sure. Whatever you need." After a lingering look at Luc's tense face, he concentrated on the necessary steps to ensure Luc's safety. The need to soothe and reassure surged through him, but it would have to wait. Keeping him safe was paramount, and he wasn't about to let Luc's fear distract him.

With the task completed, he smiled. "There. All done."

"I-I'm n-not—"

"Hey!" He slid his hand around Luc's jaw, cupped his face, and locked in eye contact. "I'm right here. I'll be holding the end of this rope. And I *will* keep you safe."

Luc's intense stare bored into him as if searching for an answer to a vital question. Would Luc place his trust in him or would his fear win? He held his breath and waited for the verdict. Somehow, his intention of enjoying things with Luc for however long it lasted had morphed into...more. The details of his plans for the future faded and blurred around the edges. And this moment—this decision, wasn't only about rock climbing.

"Okay." The softly whispered word hung between them as Luc leaned into the hand Rick still clasped around his jaw. Luc's body sagged, turning heavy and pliant as if handing over complete trust and control of his body and well-being.

*Damn.* Powerful feelings surged through Rick at the physical signs of Luc's surrender and trust. So many conflicting and confusing emotions. He wanted to devour Luc's mouth—to dominate and take control, reassure and soothe.

He drew in a ragged breath. "Okay. You can do this." He leaned in and rested his lips against Luc's temple. "I've got you. I'll keep you safe and never let you down."

Luc grabbed Rick's shirt, his white-knuckled grip crushing the material, before he chuckled, released his hold, and took a step back. "I hope you'll let me down at some stage. I really don't want to stay up on that wall forever."

"Yes." Grinning, he clasped Luc's shoulder. "You know what I mean."

Luc smiled and lowered his gaze to the floor. "Yeah. I know. Thanks."

"Okay, then." With a final squeeze of Luc's shoulder, he turned to face the wall. "Let's go."

After a few instructions, Luc placed his foot on a green "rock" and reached out with a trembling hand to grasp his first handhold. Rick was so damn proud of Luc for attempting to conquer his fear, he didn't care if he made it to the top or only part of the way. The trust he had placed in him already made the day a success.

With a firm hold on the safety rope, he watched Luc's halting progress. "Just remember to push up with your legs. If you rely solely on pulling yourself up with your arms, you'll run out of strength before you reach the top."

"Okay."

Luc slowly but surely climbed higher, pausing at each successful step before choosing his next stepping-stone and handhold. Rick couldn't stop smiling as he kept the safety rope taut and tracked Luc's progress, so proud and amazed, once again, by Luc's willingness to do what he asked. The sweetest thrill had been when Luc had leaned into him and whispered "Okay," agreeing to accept his guidance and give over his trust.

Rick had never before had that in a relationship. His previous relationships had been brief and unsatisfying and based on two independent, like-minded men sharing a physical attraction. None of them had ever *needed* him, and they wouldn't ever have stood for the type of dynamic developing between him and Luc. The men he had dated would have thought it made them weak or...less to accept help or lean on him emotionally.

As he watched Luc near the top of the wall, he held his breath. Only one more "rock" should do it. With his focus fixed on Luc, his heart hammering, he waited as Luc hugged the wall, motionless. Why had he stopped? Had he pushed Luc too hard? Was he too exhausted to continue? Or too terrified? Damn it, maybe he should have told him to take it easy for his first time and only aim for halfway. It was too—

His breath caught.

Luc reached up, gripped the highest red rock, and pulled himself up to the top of the wall. After taking a second to steady himself, he turned his head to look down, his smile beaming.

Rick had no words. None. His awe of Luc left him speechless. To hell with technique, Luc had done it. And that smile...

With his own smile wide enough to make his cheeks ache, he gave Luc a thumbs-up and stood staring and grinning for a few seconds until Luc called out.

"Ah, Rick? What now?"

*Oh, damn. I need to guide him down.* "Okay, keep facing the wall. Remember what I told you about letting go. I'll lower you with the rope, and you abseil down, pushing your feet against the wall as you go."

Luc's smile disappeared.

"It's okay, Luc. I've got you. You can do it." His gut clenched as he pulled against the taut rope and braced his legs, ready for Luc to begin his descent. He had every faith in the equipment and his ability to guide Luc down, but he knew Luc must be terrified of releasing his hold on the rocks and allowing the harness to bear his full weight.

A few tense moments later, Luc finally let go of the wall and transferred his hands to the rope. Rick braced for action and smoothly lowered him toward the ground. Luc handled the descent like a pro, swinging out from the wall before swinging back inward and bracing his feet against the wall again. Once his brave soon-to-be lover had landed, Rick released the rope and hugged him, harness and all.

Luc gave a shaky laugh. "I can't believe I just did that."

"Well, I *can* believe it. You're amazing." After an extra squeeze, he loosened his hold and leaned back. "Are you glad you did it?"

Luc's smile lit up the room. "Yes! I never would have thought I could do that."

"You did it. It was all you."

"No, it was you." He placed his hand on Rick's chest, his palm over Rick's heart. "I couldn't have done it alone, and I wouldn't have thought to attempt this with anyone else."

Staring into Luc's eyes, he leaned down until their lips almost touched. "We make a good team."

"Yeah. We do."

"There's something else we do well together."

"Mmm? What's that?"

"This." He brushed his lips against Luc's oh-so-tempting mouth, teasing him with barely there pressure until Luc moaned and clutched at his shirt. Rick reluctantly broke the kiss. "It's time I took you home."

"Wha— Why?" Luc appeared dazed and confused.

Rick slid his hand over Luc's shoulder, and then slowly down over his chest, pausing at the harness fastening. "We have to celebrate your climbing success."

"H-how?"

He stared into Luc's eyes as he unfastened and removed the harness, punctuating each confident action with his words. "In the very. Best. Way."

# Chapter Sixteen

LUC'S APARTMENT DOOR had barely closed before his back hit the wall. "Oomph!"

With a guttural growl, Rick ground his hips against Luc, trapping him in place. In a flurry of arms and hands and impatient curses, Rick's shirt disappeared.

Luc groaned. Oh, yeah, the friction of Rick's denim-covered dick, rubbing and grinding, was enough to drive a man insane. On the ride home, he had feared he would come in his pants like a teenager, just thinking about the promise of Rick's words, the way he had removed the harness—manhandled him. *Fuck*. And now, Rick's bare chest—a masterpiece of color and texture. All hard muscle and smooth, tanned skin, accented by the perfect amount of dark hair. His gaze flicked between Rick's nipples. With his breathing ragged, he slid his hands up Rick's chest. Hair tickled his fingers and palms. He paused, his hands flat and fingers splayed—a mere twitch away from touching the brownish-pink discs of flesh.

Quivers ran through his belly as Rick's hands cupped his ass. *Dear God*. Those large hands engulfing his ass cheeks were enough to turn his brain to mush. With one firm grip of those hands, he forgot about the world around him. Day, night, public, private—nothing mattered except the pressure and slide of those twin instruments of bliss. And when they squeezed—

"Ahh." His hips jerked forward, mashing his cock against Rick's thigh. Pure unadulterated ecstasy. As Rick latched onto his neck, biting and licking and sucking, all while gripping and kneading his ass, goose bumps tingled and danced across Luc's skin. He moaned and writhed, twining his arms around the big man's neck, clinging like a vine to a giant oak.

With biceps bulging, Rick hoisted him higher and spun around, reversing their positions until Rick's back leaned against the wall. When Luc's feet were firmly on the ground again, he tugged at Rick's hair until Rick transferred his attention from his neck to his mouth.

A sigh escaped as surprisingly soft lips pressed against his in a gentle caress. Shivers danced up the back of his head. He loved that such a towering, strong man could be so gentle—so caring. With each slide of his lips, Rick's whiskers tickled his mouth, his cheek, his nose. Before Rick, he had never kissed anyone with a beard. It added new sensations. He liked it.

Want. Need. As much as he appreciated the gentleness, he wanted Rick to manhandle him again.

And he *needed* Rick to be in control.

As if reading his mind, Rick swiped his tongue across the seam of Luc's lips, demanding they part.

*How can I refuse?*

At the barest opening of his mouth, Rick surged inside, his tongue bold and demanding, sending Luc's head into a spin and his knees shaking, forcing him to cling to Rick's neck. His lover's movements were commanding. His hands, chest, arms—everything was massive and strong and sexy as hell. Rick's kiss claimed him—dominated him, Rick's arms and body surrounding and overwhelming him, allowing no escape. Barely allowing him to breathe.

*Hell, yeah! Exactly like that.*

Rick nipped Luc's lips and kneaded his ass before releasing his mouth. "You like that?"

They both knew what he meant. And yes, he liked it. A lot. Gasping, he drew in deep breaths. "Yes."

Shivers raced up his spine as rough hands divested him of his shirt and wrenched his jeans open. He moaned as Rick plunged his giant paw—*hand*—into his briefs and engulfed his cock, the firm strokes making his flesh throb. He needed to touch Rick. Now.

Panting into Rick's mouth, he fumbled with Rick's button and zipper. They just...wouldn't cooperate. With a frustrated huff, he dragged his lips from Rick's talented mouth and looked down at the tricky fastenings between their bodies. And almost came. The sight and sensation of Rick's fingers encircling his leaking cock, Rick's thumb smearing precome across the tip and pressing on the slit pushed him close to the edge. *Oh, God.* He rested his forehead against Rick's solid chest and drew in a few more deep breaths.

*I'm going to last. I'm going to last, but... Fuck!*
*Okay, focus.*

The button beneath his fingers finally came free, and he unfastened and shoved Rick's jeans down past his muscular thighs. Unfettered, Rick's thick, cut cock bounced free, slapping against his stomach. Luc's mouth went dry.

*Everything* about Rick was massive.

Luc's ass clenched and fluttered. Would it fit? Perhaps he should start with trying to swallow it. He desperately wanted to taste it. Falling to his knees, he stared at the long, rigid flesh. Was it too big or just right? He smiled and licked his bottom lip. Well, it certainly looked sizeable. But too large?

Never.

He swiped his tongue across the tip, savoring the burst of salty flavor, before sliding his gaze upward. Over Rick's taut abs and his fur-covered chest until he locked in eye contact with beautiful brown eyes.

Rick swallowed, slid his hands into Luc's hair, and cradled his head. "Do it." His fingers twitched, urging Luc's head toward his groin.

*Yes!* He gripped the base of Rick's cock and then swallowed it whole—well, half of it. With his lips stretched wide, and the cockhead bumping the back of his throat, he fought the urge to gag. He was no novice, but Rick was…endowed. He pulled back to breathe and swallow repeatedly, generating saliva before trying again.

This time, he beat the gag reflex, swallowing convulsively around the smooth cockhead. Long and thick, rock-hard muscle sheathed in soft, silky skin filled his mouth. His eyes watered, and a tear rolled down his cheek. Rick's growl of pleasure sent vibrations through Luc's mouth, reward enough, but when Rick slid his fingers over his scalp, petting and clutching before thrusting his cock deep into his throat, a warm glow flooded Luc's chest.

He had *pleased* Rick Masters. *His* Master.

*What the hell?* He wrenched free, releasing the pulsing flesh with a wet plop. Where the hell had that thought come from? His heart thundered against his ribs as he raised his startled eyes to Rick.

In all his hulking glory, Rick leaned against the wall, head thrown back and eyes closed. *Beautiful.* Luc's heart settled. The "Master" thought had kind of freaked him out, but in some crazy way, kneeling at Rick's feet felt *right*. Being submissive didn't really appeal.

*Liar, liar.*

Well, he still wasn't sure that's what this was—*pants on fire*—but he couldn't deny how much he liked Rick ordering him around and taking control.

And he wanted to please Rick some more. Right now.

Rick's eyelids fluttered before opening wide. "Shit!" He jerked Luc to his feet and cradled him in his arms. "Did I hurt you? I'm so sorry. I shouldn't have thrust. I tried not to, but... Damn, I'm so sorry."

Luc blinked in confusion, and another tear escaped. "What?"

"I'm sorry." Rick cradled the back of Luc's head with his palm, leaned in, and licked the tear from his cheek before brushing his lips against the corner of his water-filled eye. "It was so good; I got carried away. I'm sorry, baby."

Warmth pooled in Luc's chest. Such a gentle giant. He grinned. "Did you just call me 'baby'?"

Rick's mouth opened and closed a couple of times. "What? I'm worried I hurt you, and that's all you can say?"

Luc kissed Rick's bristle-covered chin before trapping his cock between their bodies. "You didn't hurt me. It felt good." He lowered his gaze to Rick's chest and fixated on a pebbled nipple. "In fact, I want you to do it again." He licked at the tempting nub of flesh. "And again. And again."

Rick groaned. "Promise me you'll tell me if I ever hurt you. I'm...big."

Luc bit his bottom lip before punctuating each word with a nip to Rick's chest. "Yes. You. Are."

Rick gasped and his cock twitched and pulsed, hitting Luc's abs with each sharp scrape of teeth. Rick growled. "Promise me!"

"Okay." He fell to his knees again and grasped Rick's cock. "I promise to tell you if you hurt me with your gigantuous pole."

Rick's laugh morphed into a strangled gurgle as Luc swallowed him down again.

Luc worshiped Rick's cock with a long, slow swipe from base to tip, before circling the smooth head with his tongue. Rick's labored breaths spurred him on, and he probed the weeping slit for nectar, savoring every taste and texture—salty, sweet, musky, rigid, and smooth. *Delicious. Better than any fantasy.* As he drew Rick's flesh deeper into his mouth, forcing it to the back of his throat, his eyes refilled with water.

*Water—not tears.* Were they triggered by the physical sensation of fullness, or could they be emotional? Well, shit, he didn't really care. So long as Rick didn't worry or fuss, he would simply ignore them.

And enjoy the moment.

The muscles beneath his wandering hands tightened, and fingers clutched his head, twisting in his hair. Rick was close. He wanted Rick to thrust into his mouth and come down his throat, but Rick's hips remained immobile. Stubborn man. Well, he wasn't about to hold back because of a bit of watery eye. Luc doubled his efforts, pushing deeper, sucking harder, and swirling his tongue over sensitive places.

"Oh, God." Rick thumped the wall with his fist and growled, but his hips remained motionless.

Luc sandwiched his hands between Rick and the wall. It seemed he would have to try harder to break the man's control. With a firm grip, he clasped the two muscular ass cheeks and jerked Rick forward, forcing the fat, meaty flesh deep into his throat.

"Ahhh!" Rick clutched Luc's head and thrust, breaking free from his self-imposed restraint.

And thrust again.

And once again.

"Fuuuck!" Rick's roar echoed throughout his body, vibrating through Luc's mouth.

Warm wetness shot down the back of his throat, forcing his reflexes to kick in. He swallowed repeatedly, constricting Rick's cockhead and milking every last drop from the pulsating flesh. So good. With trembling hands, he skimmed over Rick's ass and thighs, soothing and calming as Rick's hips jerked erratically.

Gasps filled the air.

Gradually, the taut ass muscles relaxed beneath his strokes. Gentle fingers slid through his hair, caressing and scratching at his scalp, before tugging and urging him to stand. He reluctantly released Rick's flesh with one last suck and swirl before pushing to his feet.

Rick kissed the corner of Luc's eye and then licked at the stray drop of water. "Mmm, so good. You okay?"

"Yeah. More than." His voice rasped. Well, he had just had a tree trunk shoved down his throat.

"That was..." Rick audibly swallowed. "I can't..."

"Yeah, I know what you mean." Curling his arms around Rick's sweat-slick body, Luc pressed his still-hard cock against him. Strangely, despite his obviously aroused-to-the-point-of-bursting cock, he was satisfied by pleasing Rick and making him come. For a while, he had forgotten about his own needs, but now...

Rick's hand circled Luc's throat, his thumb toying with his Adam's apple.

Luc's cock pulsed, and a shiver ran through him, the instinct to fall to his knees almost overwhelming. "Oh, God."

Rick's lips brushed the skin of Luc's neck, beneath his jaw. "You still have your pants on. We need to remedy that."

"Wha—what?"

"I want my mouth on you." Rick swirled his tongue around Luc's Adam's apple, two delicious licks of the sensitive mound that made them both groan, before he pulled back and locked in eye contact. "Pants off. Now!"

Luc's breath hitched.

*Oh, yes, Sir.*

# Chapter Seventeen

EYES CLOSED, LUC lay on the couch beside Rick with his upper body sprawled across the big man's bare chest. Like a boneless puppet, pliant to his master's maneuverings, Luc's heavy limbs remained precisely where Rick had placed them. He had no desire to move and could happily stay there for the rest of his life. *Please?* As his lover's heart slowed to a comforting rhythm beneath his cheek, Luc's rasping breaths gradually eased.

"You good?" With a long, slow stroke, Rick caressed the back of Luc's head, his fingers swirling in the short hairs at the base of his skull before repeating the soothing motion.

Stroke, swirl. Stroke, swirl.

Tingles ran across Luc's skull and down his spine. "Mmm, goo—"

The deep rumble of Rick's chuckle vibrated against his ear. He should probably try to say something else—use actual words to convey how amazing that experience had been. How he loved that Rick had manhandled—dominated him. And how he'd never felt anything as powerful as that moment, kneeling, his mouth stretched to the limit by Rick's cock, that instant when his lover lost control. Because of him.

The only experience that compared came a few minutes later as Rick returned the favor, surrounding his dick with the hot, wet heat of his mouth. But he just couldn't articulate... That was... Rick was...

"Yeah." Rick kissed the top of his head. "Sleep now."

*Well, okay, maybe just a short nap.*

*Gasoline fumes burned his sinuses. Red-and-white lights flashed, illuminating the night like a kaleidoscope of fractured images. Crushed metal. Voices. A deafening roar and shooting sparks.*

*Hands reaching for him.*

Luc jerked awake, his heart hammering as he fought to free himself from the effects of the images.

"Hey. Are you okay?"

Hard muscles shifted against his cheek, and arms encircled him, holding him close. The fog began to dissipate from his brain, and his senses sharpened.

*Rick. I'm on the couch with Rick.*

"Luc?" Rick slid his hand upward, leaving a trail of warmth across Luc's skin before covering the back of his head with his massive hand, pressing Luc's face into warmth and strength.

*The same as that night.*

"Luc? You were dreaming."

"Yeah."

"You were pretty agitated."

"Sorry."

"Do you want to talk about it?"

With his nose pressed against Rick's chest, he inhaled deeply, allowing the musky, manly scent to envelop and overwhelm him, blocking out everything but the strong man who held him. Nothing existed outside the warm, safe embrace.

*The same as that night.*

His heart rate slowed, and he exhaled. "It was the car accident. I haven't dreamed about it for years."

"Your parents' car accident?"

"Yes, but I was there too."

"Shit. I didn't realize." Rick caressed Luc's head. "You said you were six or seven years old?"

"Six."

"Damn. Were you hurt?"

"A few scrapes and bruises. It was a long time ago." The rhythmic strokes against the back of his head soothed and calmed. "That feels nice. He did that too."

The stroking paused. "He?"

"The paramedic—fireman, I can't remember which one he was. He pulled me from the wreck."

Rick resumed his caresses, his fingers burrowing beneath Luc's hair to scratch his scalp. "You can remember that?"

"Yes. He was big. Strong. I remember clinging to him as if my life depended on it. I felt like... If I let go of him, I'd be lost. They tried to pull me away, put me into the ambulance, but I wouldn't let them. His size, his body and arms, were like a cocoon, blocking out the noise and lights and chaos as they continued cutting into the car to retrieve..." He drew in a deep breath and pushed the pain away. "I focused on him. I didn't want to think about what was happening. He held me all the way to the hospital. His strength and his warmth were... He was...safety."

Rick rolled Luc onto his back and hovered over him, his mouth mere inches from Luc's lips. "I'm so sorry." He shook his head. "It's crazy, but I wish... I wish it could have been me, holding you, protecting you."

"You're here now. And it was a long time ago."

"That's what you said before."

"Yeah. It's what I always say."

Rick studied him, his stare intense as if he searched for meaning in things unspoken.

And in that long, silent moment, Luc began to hope that Rick would find the answers.

Rick slowly lowered his head and captured Luc's lips in a soft, lingering kiss. His lips brushing, sliding, and soothing.

*It felt like...a promise?*

A tear slid from beneath Luc's closed eyelid.

*A guy can hope.*

With a hum, his lover released his mouth and captured the falling tear with his lips before returning to their kiss. The taste of salt and sorrow seeped into the tangle of their tongues. Luc's heart rate rose, desperation building, rising through his body like a surge of energy. He clutched at Rick, his fingers digging into the hard flesh of his back. He needed to be closer, joined, merged into one entity. He had never felt anything comparable before. He surged against him and opened his mouth wider, inviting Rick to take and consume.

Strong hands held him close. Hot, hard flesh pressed him into the couch, covering him like a blanket—a barrier between him and the world. And his memories.

In the oblivion of Rick's arms, he lost himself and found peace and safety.

# Chapter Eighteen

RICK SAVORED THE warm morning sunshine against his face. Blue skies, beds of startling white flowers, and maple leaves rustling in the breeze—what more could a man ask for? Well, he could do without the hundreds of other people milling about the bustling pedestrian mall. He wasn't a fan of crowds, and he'd much rather be alone with Luc.

*Damn it.* He jerked his arm to his side as yet another child collided with one of his elbows and began crying. Before he could apologize, a glaring mother had whisked him away from the ogre. He felt bad for the child but also baffled. You'd think the sight of a giant would have them running away from him, not into him.

At least Luc seemed fine today. Relaxed. Content. After the intensity of the night before, he had wondered how Luc would react. That one image kept returning to his mind—Luc kneeling at his feet, luscious lips wrapped around his dick, a tear spilling from his eye. Taking control had felt so natural, so right, and they had pushed a few of the so-called "normal" boundaries, but Luc had taken it all and asked for more. He'd never before felt such compatibility with a partner, and the night had held a few revelations for him.

Then Luc had had that dream, and their relationship had changed again. Deepened. Hearing about the time of Luc's accident and imagining Luc as a boy, so small and vulnerable, had added to his understanding of Luc's needs.

Rick shoved his hands into his pockets and waited for Luc to finish studying the knickknacks in yet another shop's window. He shifted from one foot to the other. "See anything?"

"Mmm. No, I don't think so." Luc wandered toward a group of people surrounding a street performer. Without waiting to see or hear if the man had any talent, Luc reached into his pocket for change.

Rick chuckled and curved his hand over Luc's shoulder, drawing him closer. "You don't even know if he sings or just stands there staring at people."

"Doesn't matter."

"What? Why?"

"He's homeless, and his best friend looks hungry."

His gaze followed Luc's gesture and alighted on the shopping trolley filled with belongings and the scruffy black dog lying beside it. His gut clenched as Luc nudged his side and grinned.

*So damn appealing.*

He squeezed Luc's shoulder before releasing his hold.

After dropping more than a few coins in the blue bucket beside the tail-wagging dog, Luc turned to scan the shops on the other side of the mall. "Oh, the Kite Shop! Let's check it out. I bet Adam would love one." And he darted off again.

With a sigh, he followed Luc across the brick-paved street, still not knowing if the performer sang, danced, or juggled. It had been years since he had visited the Pearl Street Mall. Shopping was not his thing, but Luc needed to buy a birthday present for his friend Adam, so Rick had agreed to accompany him. Stupidly, he had envisaged a quick visit to a particular store, the purchase of a preplanned gift, and then a lazy hour or so sitting in a café with Luc.

So wrong.

Luc had arrived with no idea what gift to buy, and Rick's lesson in Window-shopping 101 began. Talk about torture. There seemed no rhyme or reason for the shops they visited or the direction they headed as Luc tried on hats and held up shiny things for his inspection. Rick had to admit the hats brought a smile to his lips. For God's sake, the man looked sexy in all of them. Even the beret! He soon determined the main bonus of the day was the need to constantly keep his eyes on Luc so as not to lose him in the crowd, and he was convinced Luc had deliberately poured himself into a pair of black skinny jeans to ensure he held Rick's attention.

*Love that ass.*

But Luc's seemingly illogical and directionless search left Rick baffled. He toyed with the idea of urging Luc to focus on the task, but the boundaries of their relationship were still a little blurry. Should he take control outside of the bedroom? Did Luc want that? On one hand, he didn't want to spoil Luc's fun, but on the other, their present course seemed to be headed for closing hour without finding a gift.

Luc stood beside the Kite Shop's window. "Now *this* is the perfect window display. Lots of color and interesting things to catch your eye. I'm sure we'll find Adam's present in here."

"God, I hope so."

Luc's answering smile, a little bit indulgent and a lot sexy, sent warmth through his chest.

*Okay, so perhaps the aimless wandering isn't a total waste of time.*

A bell tinkled as Luc opened the door, heralding their entrance into chaos. An explosion of color and shapes overloaded Rick's senses as he tried to focus on individual items. Kites of all sizes and designs hung from the ceiling, walls, and display racks.

Luc craned his neck to view the kites above. "Oh, my God. I love this store. I can't believe I didn't think of coming here first."

Rick gave a silent groan. *Oh, how I wish you had* was on the tip of his tongue, but Luc's beaming smile halted his complaint.

Luc had great smiles.

"Look at this one. And this." Luc darted between display racks to examine and touch what seemed like every kite in the store. "Look, they have ones from my favorite animated TV series." Luc pointed to the display on the wall.

"Okay. That's...good?"

Luc cocked his head and gave him the evil eye. "Please tell me you recognize those characters, because if you don't, I will immediately stop shopping and go home."

"Is that a trick threat?" He raised an eyebrow. "Because I'm not seeing the downside of not knowing who—or what, that is."

"You don't know?" Luc's last word hit a higher octave.

"They look sort of familiar, but no, not really."

"It seems I'll have to educate you." Luc grabbed his hand and headed toward the wall display.

"Wait, what about your threat to go home? If you don't follow through, I'll never trust you again."

"No way, I'm not letting you off that easy. And after I've shown you these, there's a whole section of sci-fi-themed kites over there." Luc grinned cheekily and pointed toward the back of the store.

"Great." Rick tried to grimace, but couldn't stop his mouth from forming a smile.

As he trailed Luc around the store, his mood began to lighten with each of Luc's comments and expressions. He marveled at Luc's enthusiasm and his ability to converse with strangers, including them in his quest for a gift as if they were old friends. And he couldn't help but notice every one of them walked away happy.

As he stared at Luc chatting with yet another person—an elderly lady whose curious gaze repeatedly flicked between him and Luc—the corners of Rick's mouth curved upward. Again. Yes, Luc wanted and needed him to take control of their physical interactions, and he may even need a nudge to focus a little more, but seeing Luc like this, so relaxed and happy was...perfect.

"Rick? What do you think?" Luc held up a rainbow-colored kite. "Susan agrees it would suit Adam's flamboyance perfectly."

"Ahh." Rick's focus shifted between the kite with a squiggly design of who knew what across the surface and the elderly woman, presumably named Susan. "Yeah. Sure."

The woman patted Luc's arm. "I'll leave you to it. The grandchildren will be waiting for me."

Luc pointed to her shopping bag. "They'll love those. Have fun."

"Thank you. You too." She moved to Rick's side, touched his arm, and whispered loudly, "Don't let him get away. That boy's a keeper." With a smile and a wink, she walked away.

Rick blinked. Well, that was interesting.

Luc's arm bumped him. "So, umm, she was nice."

Rick watched, fascinated as a rosy flush crept up his lover's neck, spread over his cheeks, and turned the tips of his ears fiery red. "Mmm." He arm-bumped Luc in return. "And correct. I always respect the advice of elders."

Luc's shy smile and lowered gaze sent his cock a-twitching. *So damn sexy.*

He curved his hand around the back of Luc's neck and rubbed his thumb across the flushed skin. "So, are we done here?"

"Well, I thought I'd just look at those ones ov—"

"Luc." He waited until Luc looked at him. "Do you think Adam will like that one?"

"Yes." Luc bit his lip and nodded. "Okay. Yes, I'll buy this one."

"Good." He gave Luc's neck a gentle squeeze. "I want to go someplace quieter."

"Yeah." Luc leaned into Rick's hold in that oh-so-trusting way. "Me too."

"Go pay for the kite." He growled against Luc's temple. "Make it quick. I have plans."

Luc's breath hitched, and he froze for a few seconds before spinning away and racing toward the cashier.

Rick grinned. No, he definitely didn't want Luc to change.

But helping him focus could be beneficial. And fun.

# Chapter Nineteen

RICK MANEUVERED THROUGH the Saturday morning traffic as smoothly as the jazz sliding from the truck's speakers. A quick glance at Luc reassured him all seemed well. A week had passed since they had spent time together. A very long week of working on surveys situated away from the city. Beside him, Luc occasionally turned to look at something that caught his attention, but he appeared calm and relaxed. And he hadn't asked where they were headed, seemingly content to trust in Rick and go wherever he had planned.

The lip biting began as they neared the outer limits of suburbia. The leg jiggling and heel tapping kicked in as soon as they turned onto the highway, heading away from the city.

Total trust still had a ways to go.

He reached over and stroked Luc's thigh. "I want to show you something—a place that's special to me."

Luc's forced smile made him sigh. *Damn.* "No hiking or abseiling involved. I promise."

"Okay." Luc's shoulders lowered, and his heel finally settled on the floor.

The farther they traveled, the scarcer houses became, but the occasional mountain retreat sat nestled amongst clusters of green or perched high on the edge of a steep slope.

In the past, he had often stopped on the side of the road and studied different styles of architecture—searching for inspiration. One time, he had knocked on the door of a particularly intriguing house to speak with the owner, a sculptor, who had been happy to show him his home and latest project.

The constant need to evaluate different design strengths and weaknesses had now passed, and he had created, molded, and formed his own vision. With each mile they traversed, heading toward the plot of land he considered his true home, Rick's excitement level rose along with the land elevation. He was eager to share his plans with Luc.

Thirty minutes later, they turned off the highway. Trees bordered the dirt driveway like a lush guard of honor, keepers of his home—his dream. He slowed the truck as they neared the end of the driveway, anticipating the moment, as always, when the tree line ceased and the vista revealed itself. His amazement and awe never grew old, and he couldn't wait for Luc's reaction.

"Wow! That's..." Mouth agape, Luc stared.

He grinned. *Yep. Speechless.*

Snow-capped mountains dominated the landscape, their white peaks reaching for a cloudless sky, fresh flurries clinging to the steep flanks. Beneath them lay a carpet of vibrant green, and thick foliage framed the view.

As the truck engine died, he sat motionless, allowing Luc to fully take in the scene.

Luc shook his head. "That view is fucking ridiculous."

"Yep. Come on." He jumped from the truck, catching hold of Luc's hand as he joined him and then towed him across the grass to the area recently leveled and pegged. "This is it."

"Mmm?" Luc's focus remained on the mountains. "I can see why this place is special to you."

With a tug on Luc's hand, he drew his attention to the level patch of ground. "And this."

Luc turned and frowned, his gaze flicking to each of the white-tipped wooden stakes surrounding them. "Is this private property?"

"It is." Unable to resist the need to touch, he draped his arm over Luc's shoulders and pulled him close. As his lover's body molded to his side, contentment settled in his chest. This place. Luc. For one perfect moment, all was right with his world. The pure mountain air filled his lungs and calmed his heart. "This is where I'm going to live."

"What?" Luc jerked out of his hold, forcing him to drop his arm.

"Yep." Smiling, he pointed to the stakes. "This is where I'll build the cabin."

"Wh-what? When?"

"Probably in a year or so."

"But if you move, what about work?"

"It's not too far to commute, and that view, this air, will make it worthwhile."

"But..." Luc's focus flicked between the pegs again. "The cabin looks so small."

"Well, it will be on the small side, but I'm not planning on building a 'tiny house on wheels' or anything."

"B-but the driveway's not paved for the winter. And what about electricity? And plumbing."

"I'll lay a driveway but connecting utilities is a major expense out here, so I'll use generators or solar, rainwater tanks, and a composting toilet."

The color leeched from Luc's face. "C-composting?"

"Yeah." Rick's smile dimmed as Luc took two steps backward, away from him. "It's all I've ever wanted. It's my dream."

"It's..." Luc bit his lip and looked around helplessly. "It's not what I was expecting," he whispered into the breeze.

"I can see that." His stomach churned. Luc looked miserable—crushed. *Damn it.* So eager to show Luc his land, his very own piece of mountain paradise, he hadn't thought about...

He hadn't thought. Full stop.

What must be running through Luc's mind? From his lover's perspective, Rick's vision of a cozy, self-sufficient cabin must seem like a primitive, isolated nightmare. He dragged his fingers across his scalp before tugging on his hair in frustration.

Buoyed by the success of the previous weekend, he had pushed too hard, too soon. It would have been better to ease Luc into the idea of this place, but instead, he had charged ahead, hoping Luc would fall in love with the site as... As what? Their future home?

*Come on, we hardly know each other.*

He stalked to the edge of the leveled land and stared at the mountains. Luc would probably *run* all the way back to the city.

Luc ghosted his hand over Rick's back as he joined him and stood at his shoulder. "I'm sorry. I reacted badly."

Rick's chest tightened at the tone of Luc's voice—regretful, almost timid. "No." He drew Luc into his arms and buried his nose in his hair. "I'm sorry. I sprung this on you without warning."

Hugging him tighter, he marveled at the way Luc rested in his arms, no awkward chest bumping or sharp bones digging into uncomfortable places. The perfect fit. If only everything were as easy as their bodies aligning. He hoped to hell that he hadn't ruined everything by bringing him here and highlighting how different they were. How different their dreams for the future were.

Luc turned in his arms to gaze at the mountains. "It really is beautiful here. Thank you for showing it to me."

The squawk of birds drew their attention to the flock passing overhead.

Luc tipped his head back to stare. "Those rotten little fuckers better not shit on us. So far I've managed not to fall on my ass or rip my clothes; I don't want bird shit splattered on my shirt."

"Or in your hair."

"Fuck no!"

Rick smiled, the constriction easing in his chest. Just a little. Luc was obviously trying to lighten the mood. "You know, you seem to swear a lot more when we leave the city."

"What can I say? All this nature crap brings out the best in me."

"Speaking of crap and bird shit, composting toilets aren't that bad. They've come a long way."

"Since when?"

"Since...a hole in the ground and a shovel?"

Luc snorted. "Great."

"Maybe I should take you to see one—give you a demo."

"Aaand the dates just keep getting better and better."

Rick smiled and brushed his lips across Luc's mouth, before reluctantly allowing Luc to pull away from him— putting distance between them.

"So, what type of wood will you use for construction?"

"Cedar, but I'll incorporate some stonework."

"Nice. What about the roof?"

"Galvanized metal, and I'll have a simple gable with a steep pitch."

"Good. Good." Nodding, Luc shoved his hands in his pockets and stared at the pegged area.

While answering more of Luc's questions about the layout of the cabin and the internal building materials he intended to use, Rick sensed a reserve—a barrier that hadn't been there before.

*Two steps forward, one step back, which is still progress. Right?*

So why did it feel like the ground was slipping away beneath his feet? He wanted to find a way to make this relationship work, but each direction held obstacles.

Some the size of mountains.

# Chapter Twenty

LUC AMBLED DOWN the corridor toward the photocopy room with thoughts of his big man running through his mind. It had been three days since he'd seen Rick, and the week dragged. Two more days until their next date. He didn't know where Rick intended to take him, but it was now clear it wouldn't be anywhere fancy. Rick seemed to prefer casual and low-key places. So, no chance of impressing Rick with intimate dinners in exclusive restaurants. Still, last week Rick had been plenty pleased and impressed with the intimacy of their *after*-dinner activities.

Wherever the destination, he hoped a composting demonstration wasn't on the agenda. A shudder ran through him. God, he couldn't think of anything worse and had been genuinely shocked at Rick's plans to live in the mountains in a rustic structure. A cozy cabin was one thing, but generators and no plumbing took things to the extreme. What would that mean for their relationship? He really couldn't imagine himself dealing with such basic amenities.

A loud thump as he passed the conference room made him pause. The open door denoted no meetings in progress. Had something, or someone, fallen? After retracing his steps, he entered the room, and—

"Rick!"

Rick grabbed him by the biceps and propelled him backward until his back hit the wall. "Rick?" No reply, just an intense stare that sent flutters through his stomach and balls. *Shit!* He licked his lips and swallowed. "Umm, I—"

Rick stepped closer, inserting one foot between his, moving closer until his thigh pressed against Luc's definitely intrigued cock. *Fuck.* Without breaking eye contact, Rick unknotted Luc's tie and slid it free from his neck. Leaning back, he grabbed Luc's hands and wrapped the red tie around his wrists. The intense, brown-eyed stare rendered Luc immobile and speechless and...hard. With two sharp yanks, the tie tightened into a knot, binding his wrists with red silk.

His heart hammered and his mouth went dry. "I don't... Wha...?"

Rick wrapped his hand around Luc's forearm, raised his bound arms, and looped them over Rick's head. The red binding lay locked against the back of Rick's neck. Hard hips shoved at Luc's groin, sandwiching him between the wall and a big, hard—

"Oh, God." His knees buckled.

The back of his head pressed against the wall as Rick smothered his mouth with a demanding kiss. He didn't know what the hell was happening, but he liked it. A lot. The scent of pine trees curled through his sinuses and blended with the taste of desire. Teeth bit his bottom lip.

"Ahh!" His lips parted as the stinging shock arrowed straight to his groin.

Rick took advantage, spearing his tongue past Luc's open lips.

Their tongues tangled.

From chest to knee, Rick's huge body ground against him. He didn't know what had brought this behavior on, *but fuck, it was good.* He dragged air into his desperate lungs through his nose. His fingers twitched with the need to touch and grasp Rick's hair, but the tie held them immobile. *Not fair!* He tugged on the restraint and whimpered.

In response, Rick slid his hands downward, caressing and kneading muscles before gripping his ass. Hard.

"Ahh!" Burying his face in Rick's neck, he panted as fingers dug into his cotton-covered flesh. "Oh, God, Rick." He licked at the salty skin, exposed by the V of Rick's shirt.

A rumble rolled through Rick's chest. "You're enough to drive a man insane. All morning you've been strolling around the office corridors. You and your sexy red tie—taunting me and everyone else. God, I want you so bad. Don't wanna lose you."

"Wha-what?" He couldn't think straight.

Rick gave Luc's ass a hard squeeze before lifting him to his toes, perfectly aligning their cocks. Luc moaned and rubbed his aching, confined flesh against Rick's hard, denim-covered ridge. He wanted to touch and lick and suck that thick cock, swallow it whole until Rick came down his throat. He needed that hard cock buried in his ass—something they hadn't done yet. Why the hell hadn't they done that yet? With a guttural groan, he ground harder against his lover.

"Luc. So damn good." Rick shifted his hold on Luc's ass, his fingers digging into the flesh beneath the conservative black trousers, the pressure parting his ass cheeks.

Fire shot through Luc's ass and curled through his balls. He latched onto Rick's neck, sucking and biting and groaning like a demented man. The world narrowed to the fingers kneading his ass and their proximity to his aching entrance. Each grip, each stinging dig of digits, moved closer, pulled wider. He wanted them to shove inside and fill him.

He hooked his foot around the back of Rick's leg and dug his heel into the hard muscle. "Please." He growled against Rick's ear. "Fuck me. With your fingers, with your cock, anything. Just fuck me."

Twin squeals of shock snapped Luc from his lust-filled haze.

He dropped his foot to the floor and peered over Rick's shoulder. Melissa and Jane, two of his coworkers, stood frozen in the corridor with their mouths gaping. *Oh, God. How could he be so stupid?* They were in a public place—his place of employment. And he—

*Oh, shit.* The beacon-red tie wrapped around his wrists screamed "Look at me!"

And they did.

Melissa's eyes widened.

*Oh, shit.*

Rick began to turn, but Luc stopped him with a jerk of his bound arms.

"Umm." Melissa cleared her throat. We were just, umm."

"We heard a noise!" Jane blurted.

Luc's face burned hotter than the fires of hell. "Yep. Sure." The tips of his ears were surely alight. "Sorry. I-I shouldn't... I don't know what I was... Sorry."

Rick growled in his ear.

With a gasp, Melissa grabbed Jane's arm, and they scuttled away down the corridor.

"Oh, God." He dropped his head onto Rick's shoulder. "What was I thinking? What must they be thinking about me? I mean, I was wrapped around you, and my tie... Oh, my, God. It can't get much worse than this. Melissa and Jane aren't gossips, but this is... Shit! What if they tell someone?" He drew in a deep breath before exhaling slowly.

His coworkers knew he was gay. He wasn't in the closet, but this would rank as unacceptable office behavior by anyone's standard.

*And it's worse because I'm the boss's nephew.*

He had always been conscious of the extra scrutiny. His colleagues could get away with the odd misdemeanor. An embarrassing kiss at the office Christmas party or inappropriate flirting was soon forgotten, but the nephew of Jeramiah Weston had his conduct held to a different standard. Unfair but true. "If it spreads, everyone will know. Oh, God. Kill me now." He would be the subject of gossip and censure for weeks.

Rick yanked Luc's arms up and pulled them from around his neck.

Luc's focus shot to Rick's face—and the murderous expression.

"I'm sorry you're embarrassed by the thought of people knowing you were with me."

"What?"

"Maybe you should tell them the uncivilized Neanderthal held you against your will and forced you to beg for a fucking."

"What?"

The muscle in Rick's jaw contracted and released before his shoulders sagged. Rick stepped back, his sad stare tearing into Luc's soul. "I guess I shouldn't have expected more."

"What?" He swallowed. Seriously? "What?" Was that all he could say?

*But what the hell is happening?*

Rick's brown-eyed gaze caressed Luc's body before settling on his eyes again. "I have to go."

Luc's stomach churned as Rick spun on his heel, strode back down the corridor, and disappeared from sight. What had just happened? He slumped against the wall. One of the hottest experiences of his life had turned embarrassing and then bewildering. Why had Rick said that stuff? He could understand Rick being embarrassed. *For God's sake, I humped him like an animal and demanded to be fucked!* So, sure, it was ridiculously embarrassing, but Rick had seemed angry and then resigned? Why? He replayed the conversation. And then replayed it again.

*Oh, hell.* He closed his eyes and sighed. *I am such an idiot. Rick thinks I'm ashamed because I was caught—with him.* That "someone like you" comment had come back to haunt him. Again.

What a disaster. Well, amazingly hot and then disastrous. Perhaps he should go back to his desk and try to get some work done, and by that, he meant stare at his computer screen pretending to work while replaying over and over what had just happened. Maybe inspiration would strike, and he could work out what to do next. He doubted things could get any worse, but—

He opened his eyes and focused on the red tie bound tightly around his wrists.

*Oh, shit.*

# Chapter Twenty-One

RICK PARKED THE truck outside the company headquarters and slumped against the steering wheel. Exhaustion pulled at his shoulders, and a throbbing pain attacked his temple like a mallet striking a survey peg. It hadn't been a particularly strenuous survey. The flat terrain and close proximity to the city had filed it under the heading of "a slow amble through the park," but his mind hadn't had a moment's rest since Thursday.

He couldn't stop thinking about Luc. The taste of Luc, the smell of his aftershave, the hardness of Luc's cock pressing against his leg. Wrapping that sexy red tie around Luc's wrists had been instinctive, and hot as hell. He wanted to do it again, along with other...stuff. His cock twitched. *Damn.* The things flashing through his mind were hot. Sexy. Kinky. Probably illegal somewhere. Luc brought out desires in him that were confusing, yet right. He didn't know how to explain it and hesitated to use the word "domination," but he loved being in control. And he loved that Luc seemed to like it too.

After drawing a deep breath and releasing it slowly, he forced himself—and his dick—to calm down. Okay, he had to face facts; Luc might be physically attracted to him, but physical attraction could only take a relationship so far. Luc's reaction—his embarrassment—said it all. Loud and clear. Luc was a certain type of guy who mixed with others of a similar kind. Rick was altogether a different type of beast—so to speak. Tony had it partly right when he said "animals" act differently when separated from their own kind, but he left out the part about how they always return to the safety and familiarity of the herd.

*Damn it. I can't believe I'm thinking about Tony's lame-ass analogies.*

After grabbing the field book from the passenger seat, he slid from the truck. Right now, he needed to forget about Luc and concentrate on business. The field book, containing the coordinates and survey calculations of the new reserve, needed to be delivered to the survey desk. In an effort to appear semi-civilized, he buttoned his blue-checked lumberjack shirt and strode through the sliding glass doors.

At the survey desk, the pretty receptionist, Mia, possibly, or Mary—he could never remember—greeted him.

"Hi, Rick. I'll just be another minute; I need to send a quick message."

"Sure."

She turned back to the computer, typed a short sentence, and then pushed send. "There." She grinned at him. "Do you have a field book for me?"

"Yes. It's a new one."

"What number please?"

"Rick Masters 307, Recreation Reserve 61492."

After adding the information to the computer, she accepted the field book with a smile. "Thanks." She glanced down the hallway and drummed her fingernails on the desk. "So, Rick, do you have any other surveys planned for this week?"

"Ah, yes." His brows drew down. For two years, he had been giving her his field books, but this was the first time she had tried to make conversation. As he wasn't one to initiate small talk, they had never moved past basic greetings and information exchange. So why now? "Tomorrow I'm surveying a small water reserve just outside Boulder."

"Oh, that's nice and close. I guess you won't need to stay overnight?"

"No, I—"

Rapid footsteps thundering down the hallway made him turn.

Luc. Form-fitting white shirt. Blue tie.

*Damn it.*

Luc skidded to a halt. "Rick! I need to talk to you." Luc smiled at the receptionist. "Thanks, Marie. I owe you one."

"No problem, Luc."

With a scowl at the traitorous *Marie* and ignoring Luc, Rick spun on his heel and headed for the exit. He really didn't want to do this here. Or now. Or ever.

Footsteps followed. "Rick, wait!"

"I believe we said enough the other day. There's no point in—"

"Stop." Luc grabbed Rick's arm, jerking him to a halt. "Please, I don't understand what's happening."

Rick glanced down at the hand gripping his forearm. He should shake it off, pull away, and show Luc he didn't want those hands on him. *Liar.* Despite the empty corridor, Rick lowered his voice. "Look, Luc. I get it. The other day we got carried away. It was hot, but now it's back to business. You in your office and me"—he waved his hand vaguely—"out there."

"No." Luc moved closer. "I need to explain."

"It's okay."

"No, it's not. I'm sorry. I said some stupid things—things I didn't mean, or at least not in the way you thought I meant."

"Okay, fine." Rick briefly closed his eyes. No, not fine, but he didn't need this and didn't want to hear explanations and justifications that probably made perfect sense to Luc, but would make *him* feel even more shitty. Luc was embarrassed to be seen with someone like him—by *being* with him. Prolonging the agony never helped. He focused on Luc's gorgeous green eyes. *Damn it.* So. Not. Fine. "It's okay, Luc. Apology accepted." With a forced, stiff smile on his lips, he tugged his arm free. "We all say stupid things that—"

"Me more than most."

Rick couldn't suppress a half smile. "Yes, especially you."

"Only around you, Rick. You have an effect on me—in more ways than one." Luc's hand hovered over Rick's bicep before dropping away. "The other day, I wasn't embarrassed about being caught with you, specifically; I was nervous about being caught...with anyone."

Rick raised his eyebrow.

Luc huffed. "Come on. You have to admit it was a pretty compromising position. Red tie bound around my wrists, your hands on my ass, me virtually climbing you and demanding to be fucked."

Rick growled and swayed closer.

Luc swallowed. "I-I hate bringing attention to myself."

"But you're the boss's nephew."

"Exactly, and I learned very early that people treat me differently. Seeing how people gossip has made me a little wary. I have to be more careful, more professional. It's unfair, but I'm held to a higher standard."

"Well." Uncertain what to think, Rick frowned and shoved his hands in his pockets. So, Luc wasn't embarrassed about *him*, not specifically, but... "But here at the office, you're so confident."

Luc ducked his head. "Am I?"

Rick opened his mouth and then closed it again. Admittedly, he had minimal office interaction with Luc on which to base that opinion, but from afar, Luc seemed confident.

Luc curled a hand around Rick's bicep and drew in a shaky breath. "Please." He pulled at his bottom lip with perfect white teeth. "Can I see you again?"

Heat coiled through Rick's groin as Luc's tongue swiped across the raw, abused lip. *Damn.* His head said "This will end badly," but his dick wanted to know why there was even a question. The memory of Luc's slim, muscular body wrapped around him, rubbing against h—

"Rick?"

Rick stared at the red, glistening lip.

"Dinner?"

He wanted to bite that beautiful lower lip.

"Coffee?"

Then he wanted to lick it better.

"A sandwich in the park? Come on, man; give me something. You're forcing me to sound desperate."

Rick dragged his gaze upward and refocused on Luc's eyes. Beautiful green eyes.

"God, Rick, you're killing me. At this stage, I'll settle for a chat in the cafeteria." Luc's focus shifted to something behind Rick, and the hand gripping his bicep slid away. Luc stepped back to stand stiffly with his hands clasped behind his back.

A tall man in a gray suit walked past them, and the soft thud of footsteps tracked the man's progress down the corridor until he turned the corner.

Rick's stomach churned as he waited for Luc to make eye contact again. "Luc, I'm trying to understand, but if that's the way you're going to react every time you see a coworker, then no. No dinner, coffee, or sandwich in the park. I respect your right to be an 'out' gay man who keeps a low profile at work, but what about when we're on a date? Will there be no touching—just in case? If we run into people from the company, will we have to pretend we're merely work colleagues? That's starting to feel like I'm being pushed back into the closet, and that's not what I've chosen to do. So, unless you can tell me that's going to change, I just can't see how..."

Luc's beautiful mouth opened and then closed again without reply.

Rick's shoulders dropped. Their lifestyles and plans for the future didn't gel, no matter how much he wanted them to. And if Luc was too ashamed to tell everyone about their relationship, he didn't see any hope. Okay, it was better this way. Cut it off before it had a chance to start—before he totally fell for Luc. A little voice whispered *too late!*

Unable to resist one last touch, he cupped Luc's jaw and rubbed his thumb across his cheek. "Bye." He dropped his hand, missing the contact already, and strode down the corridor toward the exit—away from Luc.

And he would not slow his stride, waiting for Luc to call out and stop him from leaving. No, no way. This really was the best thing for everyone. Was it overreacting? Being unfair? Maybe, but it had been stupid to start anything in the first place. And he would not linger, giving Luc more time to call out and stop him. Nope, definitely not.

Silence followed him around the corner and into the lobby.

*Damn. Looks like it really is the end.*

# Chapter Twenty-Two

SWEAT RAN BETWEEN Rick's shoulder blades as he slammed the mallet onto the peg.

*I'm an idiot.*

Why the hell had he given Luc an ultimatum?

The mallet struck the peg again like a death knell.

*What a fool.*

He had probably ruined everything. So what if Luc wasn't sure about their relationship yet? It had only been a few weeks.

*I shouldn't have tried to rush things.*

The combination of new, confusing emotions and his stupid pride were to blame. Burning-hot lust and the need to be in control had overridden his common sense, while deeper, softer feelings had snuck under his barriers, and the urge to fold Luc into his arms and his life had grown each day. The desire to reveal their relationship to everyone burned in his gut, and he wanted the world to know *right now!* And with an aching intensity, he needed Luc willing and longing and begging for it—for him. Today, not tomorrow.

Another wild swing at the peg embedded it flush with the ground.

Of course, Luc was entitled to his reservations, and he had every right to proceed cautiously. The old saying about walking in another man's shoes applied. He had no idea what it meant to be Luc—the boss's nephew and heir apparent to the company.

And now the chance to find out could be lost.

By ignoring Luc's concerns and trying to rush things, he had behaved like a demanding prick and a bully. Despite the challenges of their lifestyles—and his mountain dream—he still wanted Luc.

With a sigh, he stood up and stretched the aching muscles in his back. As he gazed out over the dry, desolate patch of newly cleared land, it seemed as if he looked into the future. This had once been a lush section of forest filled with flora and fauna, but now it resembled a lonely barren wasteland.

*Damn it.* With a flick of his arm, the mallet slammed to the ground. Okay, time to stop being a maudlin sap and do something about it. First, an apology. Second, anything and everything necessary to try to fix things between them. After grabbing his phone from his back pocket, he stared at the screen for all of two seconds before changing his mind. Bad idea. Luc deserved more than a phone-call apology. Unfortunately, that meant waiting until his return to the city in two days. For the first time, staying at the cabin while finishing a survey seemed a chore—something to be endured. Too many memories of the last time he stayed there with Luc.

After gathering his tools, he headed for the truck.

Two days.

Two very long days.

Thirty minutes later, he arrived back at the cabin to find Jack Dawson's truck parked outside. A wall of warmth hit him in the face as soon as he opened the door. His gaze flicked to the roaring fire and then to Jack standing in the kitchen, holding a coffee cup. "Hi."

"Hey, Rick."

"I thought you weren't arriving until tomorrow."

"I decided to drive up today and get an early start tomorrow morning. The job will take a full day, so I'll stay tomorrow night as well. Is that okay?"

"Of course. It's not like I'm using this place as a romantic getaway." He gave a short, sharp laugh and dumped his backpack on the floor before falling onto the couch. "No chance of that at the moment."

"Oh, oh. Trouble with Luc?"

"What? How did you know? I never told you about Luc."

"Oh, um." Jack turned away and fussed with the coffee and sugar containers. "I guess someone told me. You know how office gossip is."

"Still." He frowned. Perhaps Luc *had* told someone at work. But that didn't explain how Jack knew. Cartographers and surveyors didn't often interact. "Can you remember who?"

A spoon clattered against the sink. "No, I don't know. Hell, it was probably just Tony taking wild guesses and talking out of his ass. Don't worry about it. I'm sure no one's gossiping." Jack wiped his hands on a tea towel. "Listen, I knew you'd be here, so I brought a couple of steaks with me. Do you want one?"

"Yeah, sure. Thanks for thinking of me."

"No prob—"

The strident ring of a cell phone made them both jump. Jack grabbed his mobile phone from the bench top and stood frowning at the screen for a few seconds. "Sorry, I have to get this."

"Sure." Rick turned away to stare at the fire. Listening to other people's phone calls always seemed rude, so he tried to tune out Jack's low murmurs. He picked up an old magazine from the coffee table and flicked over a few pages, but he couldn't focus. The urge to call Luc resurfaced, but he pushed it away. He hated talking on the phone, and Luc deserved a face-to-face apology.

Jack's voice grew louder. "I told you, Adam." He glanced at Rick and turned his back. "Yes, two nights... Okay, I'll leave early... Yes, he will... Okay, I'll make sure he is... Okay, bye." Jack hung up and faced him. "Something's come up, and I won't be staying tomorrow night after all. So, you'll have the place to yourself."

"Okay. Is everything all right?"

"Yes, fine, just a slight change of plan." Jack cleared his throat. "So, you'll still be staying two nights?"

"Yes."

"So...tonight and tomorrow night and then leave early the next morning?"

"Yes, that's the plan." Rick frowned and watched Jack shift from one foot to the other. He appeared unusually agitated, very un-Jack-like. On the phone, he had said the name "Adam"; could that be the same Adam as Luc's friend?

Jack strode back into the kitchen. "How about I get the meal started? It's not too early, is it?"

"No. Now is good." He mentally shook his head. It wasn't his business if Jack knew Adam, even if they were unlikely friends. But he did care if Adam was gossiping about Luc behind his back. Perhaps that explained why Jack had been acting weird. He would mention it to Luc—after apologizing and making amends.

But first, he had to get through two more nights.

Two very long, lonely nights.

# Chapter Twenty-Three

"CAN'T THIS JALOPY go any faster?" Luc scowled and turned to stare at Adam. "I mean, seriously, you earn the same as me. Can't you buy a decent car?"

Adam's knuckles whitened as he gripped the steering wheel. "I know you're anxious to get there, but may I remind you that I'm doing you a favor. There's no need to behave like such a..." Adam shook his head and drew in a deep breath. "Anyway, according to my source, Rick is settling in for his second night at the cabin. Alone. So we don't need to break any speed limits. And if your car is so much better, why is it at the mechanic's?"

"I'm having it servi—"

"And can I remind you that not everyone has a rich uncle to buy them their luxury dream car."

"I wasn't talking about an expensive car, just something reliable, and I can't believe you said that. You know I didn't want to accept the car from Uncle J. And you were there; I could hardly refuse his gift. I would have liked to see you say no to him after he cried in front of two hundred party guests and told them how proud he was of me, and how happy it made him to give it to me."

Adam's shoulders slumped. "I know, I know."

"And you know it's the only thing I've ever accepted from him. I earn my wage, and I pay my way."

"You do, and I'm so sorry. I know how sensitive you are about it, and that was a really low blow. Shit. I am the worst friend. We promised we'd never let men or money come between us, and I'm being a total pri—"

"No." Luc sighed. Shit, he was the one being an asshole. "I'm sorry too. Really sorry. I appreciate you bringing me up here. My only excuse for being so short-tempered is that I'm stressed about this meeting with Rick. I mean, let's face it; I'm planning to ambush him, and I have no idea how he's going to react."

"If he hurts you, he'll have to deal with me."

Luc smiled. "I'd like to see that."

"I'll kick his ass."

"Are you talking about a verbal or physical ass kicking?"

"Both, although I do excel at cutting a man down to size with my razor-sharp tongue."

Luc laughed. "Okay. Now I'm picturing you clinging to Rick's back while you flay him with cutting remarks about his manhood. Is that what you had in mind?"

"Of course." Adam turned and gave him a grin.

"Well, on the physical front, I think the two of us combined would have trouble bringing the big man down, but verbally, you'd decimate him. He's not the most talkative man."

Adam snorted. "Must be a surveyor thing."

Luc raised both eyebrows. "I'm guessing there's a story behind that comment. Is there something going on between you and a certain surveyor named Jack? You know, the big guy whose ass we both ogled as he bent over in the parking lot?"

"No. No chance." Adam stared directly ahead at the road with a mulish expression. "I have it on the best authority that Jack Dawson is definitely, positively straight."

"Bummer."

"Yeah. But enough of that dead-end subject. Let's get back to kicking Rick's ass."

Luc smiled. "I think I can handle Rick, but thank you for offering and having my back."

"Hey, that's what friends are for."

"And for the record, your car is just fine."

"No, my car is not fine, and we both know it. These mountain roads are testing Old Bertha, and she sounds like she's ready to blow a gasket."

"Oh, God, I really hope she doesn't. My plan to dash into the mountains, confront Rick, sort out our issues, and then have hot and heavy makeup sex will not go well if we have to call Rick to come rescue us."

"No, not the best scenario. Tell you what; give me some more details of the hot and heavy that you intend to do to your lumberjack. It'll keep our minds off the flashing engine light and the clouds of black smoke we're leaving like a trail behind us."

"No."

"Please."

"Never."

"You're no fun. Here I am risking my only means of trans—"

"Turn right!"

"What?"

He pointed. "There! There!"

"Shit, Luc. Give a guy some warning." Adam slowed the car and pulled over on the side of the road.

"You missed the turnoff."

"I didn't even see a road."

"Well, it's more of a dirt track, but it had a signpost."

"I didn't see that either."

"It's small."

"Okay." Adam turned to face him. "So is this dirt track long? Can you walk to the cabin?"

"It's not long, so yeah, I guess."

"Well, if you want to surprise Rick, it's probably best I don't drive Old Bertha down that track to the house. All the engine screeching and exhaust farting will be a dead giveaway that someone's coming."

"True."

"And she's made it this far on paved roads, so I don't want to tempt fate by going off road."

"Fair enough."

"And if she breaks down—"

"It's okay, Adam. Here is fine."

"Well, okay. But I'll wait here for an hour." He patted the dashboard. "She could do with a little rest, and if things don't go well with Rick, I can still take you home."

"Okay. Sounds like a good plan." After inhaling deeply and then releasing it slowly, he unbuckled his seat belt. "Wish me luck?"

"Of course. Go give him hell for making unreasonable demands."

"Mmm."

"Hey! None of that wishy-washy 'mmm' stuff. Remember what I told you. Tell him off. Don't let him distract you. And don't let him steamroll or bully you."

He frowned. "No, he wouldn't. Rick's not like that at all."

Adam raised an eyebrow.

"He's not. He's actually pretty sweet."

"Sweet?"

"Well, perhaps 'sweet' isn't the correct word, but he's...caring."

"Yeah, sure, when he's not giving ultimatums."

"Mmm." Luc bit his lip and stared out the window.

"Okay, sorry, positive input only. So, tell him how you feel. Be strong. Say what you need to say, and don't let him interrupt. Okay?"

"Yeah." He sat up straighter. "Yes. Definitely."

Adam slapped Luc's leg. "Yes. Go get him!"

"Yes!" Luc grinned. He could do this.

"And tell him to keep the demanding and bossy attitude where it belongs—in the bedroom."

"Adam! Please!"

"What?"

Luc shook his head and climbed from the car.

*I really should stop telling Adam my fantasies.*

# Chapter Twenty-Four

LUC STRODE DOWN the rough dirt track toward the cabin. Would Rick be inside or out hiking? Either way, he wasn't leaving until he gave Rick a piece of his mind.

*And then a piece of my ass.*

He grinned and jumped over a deep hole. Probably the hole responsible for giving him a goose egg on his forehead. His smile fell. Hopefully this trip would be injury free and have a happy ending.

At the end of the track, he stopped to stare at the cabin. Rick's truck stood out front, and smoke curled from the chimney. Both good signs. He mounted the wooden steps and wiped his sweaty palms on his jeans while staring at the cabin door. This was it. Rick was on the other side of that rustic wooden door. He pulled his shoulders back and stood straighter.

*Okay, tell him how I feel. Don't let him interrupt.*

He drew in a deep breath. *Okay, here goes nothing.*

He rapped on the door three times and waited. Was Rick home? His gaze strayed to the right to the brass bell. Grasping the dangling rope, he gave it a sharp tug. The loud clang echoed through the woods, startling birds from trees and sending God knows what kind of furry critters scuttling into hiding.

"All right, all right, I'm coming! You'd think—"

The door flew open.

Rick raised an eyebrow. "Luc?"

Rick's broad, bare chest filled the doorway. *Oh, yeah.* Perfect tanned skin just waiting to be touched and kissed. *And that sexy chest hair!*

Luc licked his very dry lips. "Like a bear," he murmured.

"Pardon?"

*Shit! Act like you didn't just say that.* "Rick, I need to talk to you." His gut clenched as Rick frowned. Angry bear.

"I thought you said it all the other day."

Luc shook his head. "No, I didn't. I need to—"

A rustling in the bushes beside the porch made him jump. "Look, can we take this conversation inside?"

Rick grunted but opened the door and stood back to let him enter.

A quick scan of the cabin's interior revealed a fire crackling merrily in the stone fireplace and the soft strains of music emitting from a small Wi-Fi speaker on the coffee table. Luc shoved his hands in his pockets and rocked on his heels before turning to Rick again. "This is nice."

Rick frowned. "Let's cut the chitchat and get right to it. I want—"

"Chitchat?" His heart began to pound. Rick's attitude grated on his nerves. *Who does Rick think he is? Chitchat? Where does he get off acting like a...* Heat raced up his neck, and he clenched his teeth. *Acting like an emotionless asshole.* "Listen, that day, you basically gave me an ultimatum and two seconds to think about it. Announce 'us' to the world or get lost."

"I know, I—"

"Yes, you did, and that's not right or fair. I mean, what are we? Is there even an 'us' to announce? You say you respect my choices."

"I do, and I'm s—"

"But if I want to explore this 'thing' between us, I have to immediately change the way I live my life to your way, embracing composting toilets and fucking each other in the hallways at work. But what if I tell everyone tomorrow and next week it's over? Why do I have to do things your way immediately? I'm not saying I'll never tell people about us, but how do I know you're worth the hassle?" He dragged air into his desperate lungs as his heart threatened to bash its way out of his chest. "If this develops into a real relationship, then I'll happily tell everyone at work, but how do I know you're not just some asshole looking for a few fucks, and then you'll dump me? Hey." He jabbed Rick in the chest with his forefinger. "What then? Tell me."

Rick moved closer. "Well, when you put it like that."

"Yeah." He jabbed Rick again because... Well, he wanted an excuse to touch that beautiful hair-covered chest. Who wouldn't?

Rick curled his hands around Luc's biceps. "I'm sorry. I guess we don't really know each other or where this is going."

Luc trailed his finger downward over taut, warm skin. "Exactly. Why would I make some grand announcement based solely on a couple of mind-altering blow jobs and a hot session of dry humping in the office conference room?"

"Well, when you put it like that." A slow smile curved over Rick's face. "Perhaps you need more material to base your decision on."

# Chapter Twenty-Five

LUC'S BACK HIT the wall. "Oomph!"

Holding Luc's wrists above his head, Rick pressed him against the wall with his body. "I can see I'll have to do more to convince you of my good intentions." He swooped in to taste the side of Luc's neck, starting at the juncture of shoulder and neck, working his way upward. Guided by Luc's moans and whimpers, he mapped his northerly course, lingering at the areas that elicited a strangled groan or a gasp. Sensitive areas deserved further exploration and extra attention.

Luc squirmed, resisting the pressure of Rick's hold. "Rick, we need to talk this through."

"Later." He buried his nose in Luc's hair and inhaled deeply. *I missed this.*

"N-no. Now."

He sighed and pulled back. His boy was a talker. "Fine. You were right. I was a dick."

"I-I... Yeah, you were."

He raised an eyebrow and stared at Luc.

Luc swallowed. "You were unreasonable and ir-rational."

"I was. I'm sorry."

"You should be."

He raised his eyebrow higher.

Luc swallowed again. "And if we're going to t-try this, you better not do anything like that again. Okay?"

"Mmm." With a growl, he leaned in and bit into the soft flesh of Luc's earlobe.

Luc's body jerked. "Ahh!"

He grinned and pressed Luc's wrists firmly against the wall beside his head. "How about that? Can I do that?"

Luc whimpered. "Mmm."

Rick rubbed his beard against Luc's cheek before scraping his teeth across the edge of his jaw. "What about that?"

"Oh, God."

"Are my intentions any clearer?"

Luc's chest heaved as he dragged air into his lungs. "I think you're head...heading in the right direction."

"Good." Rick locked in eye contact. "I missed you."

"Yeah, me too."

The corner of Rick's mouth curved upward. "Glad that's sorted. Now..." He swooped in for a quick, hard kiss before pulling away with a groan. "Stay. Right there. Don't move."

"O-okay."

Releasing his hold, he backed away. Luc stayed, back to the wall and spread-eagled.

*Damn, that's hot.* He couldn't describe what it did to him to see Luc pinned to the wall by his words. After one last searing look, he strode into the bathroom, grabbed a towel and supplies, and returned to the living room. He draped the towel over the back of the couch and tossed the lube and condoms on the seat. All ready. Now all he needed...

Luc stood splayed against the hallway wall, panting, eyes pleading.

*So damn gorgeous.* Rick unbuckled his belt. "Come here." His cock hardened as Luc obeyed. "Now, strip for me."

Luc sprang into action, a mass of frenzied arms and legs. A shirt button flew off and skipped across the floor as Luc's belt and jeans hit the floor. Luc bent over and then lurched forward, his feet caught in his jeans. "Shit."

Rick caught him before he could face-plant on the floor. "Easy now."

Luc clutched at Rick's biceps. "Shit, that wasn't supposed to happen. I'm such a klutz, and we aren't even in the great outdoo—"

"Shhh." He leaned in and sucked on Luc's bottom lip. "No talking. The only sounds I want to hear from you are moans and groans." He splayed his fingers over the back of Luc's head, cupping his skull and kissing him, long and deep.

Luc whimpered.

Rick whispered against Luc's lips. "And that. I like that sound."

"Yes, Sir."

"Fuck! And that." Plundering Luc's mouth, he sucked and devoured as if he was starving. And he was. He couldn't get enough of the taste and feel and sound of his lover. His hunger would never be sated.

Lack of air finally forced them apart.

Luc clutched Rick's shirt in his fists, his face flushed. "So, to be clear. Moans, groans, whimpers, and 'Yes, Sir' are permitted."

"And begging."

"Begging?"

"Mmm." He nuzzled Luc's neck. "Anything that resembles begging is allowed."

Luc groaned and tipped his head, giving Rick easier access. "Like 'please'? 'More'? 'Hell, yeah'?"

Rick nipped at Luc's neck.

Luc jerked. "Ahh!"

"Exactly." Rick soothed the hurt with his tongue, holding the trembling man closer against his chest. If he wasn't mistaken, Luc was in danger of collapsing on the floor in a heap. "Any and all of the above, with variations, will be acceptable."

"O-okay."

"Good. Now, get those pants from around your ankles."

Trapped in Rick's arms, Luc wriggled and kicked until he stood, as ordered, wearing only his boxers.

"Good, now..." He slid both hands over Luc's head, burrowing his fingers into the silky hair, his fingernails dragging across his scalp. The clean aroma of citrus shampoo invaded his senses, before he gripped Luc's hair and yanked his head backward. Luc's gasp sent quivers through his belly and tightened his balls. There was something about being fully dressed and having Luc near naked, pliant and at his mercy...

For a moment, he stared at Luc's startled, open mouth, lips glistening with saliva, enticing him. He leaned down and nipped at the plump flesh.

Luc sighed. "Please."

Rick growled against Luc's mouth. "Please what?"

Luc trembled. "Please, *Sir*."

"Good boy." He spun Luc around, and with a hand between Luc's shoulder blades, he bent him over the back of the couch and pinned him down by the neck. "Stay."

Luc whimpered.

Rick's breath hitched. Was that a good whimper, or God forbid, a scared whimper? Had his actions been too rough? Gone too far? Damn it, they should have discussed a safe word or something. He eased his hold. "Babe? You okay?"

"Hell, yeah." Luc wiggled his ass.

"Okay." He laughed, but released Luc's neck and slid his hands over the taut muscles of Luc's back. Long, slow strokes from his shoulders to the top of his ass.

Luc wiggled his ass again.

Rick grinned and delivered a sharp smack to the cotton-covered cheek.

"Ow!"

"Stop being demanding."

"I didn't say anything." Luc wiggled.

*Smack! Smack!*

Luc moaned and pushed his ass back toward Rick.

Rick skimmed his hands over the curves. "Like that, do you?" He delivered another smack, which stung his palm. Warmth radiated through the cotton boxers. His cock pulsed. He wanted to see that rosy-red ass cheek. With a hard yank, he stripped the underwear over Luc's ass and down to his ankles.

Pink, hot skin filled his hands. Groaning, he squeezed the firm flesh before trailing his knuckles down the shadowy cleft. Flesh quivered beneath his fingers as he headed southward, whispering over sensitive skin, before brushing and cupping Luc's balls. So damn sexy.

Luc whimpered and clawed at the couch cushion.

The blood rushed from Rick's head to his cock. Fully dressed didn't cut it. In ten seconds flat, his clothes were gone and his aching hardness bobbed free. Surging forward, he pressed his cock along the crease of Luc's ass and thrust, rubbing his cockhead across Luc's entrance.

"Ahh! Oh, God. Please." Luc pushed back and panted.

"Soon." He grabbed the lube and squeezed a generous dollop down the crease of Luc's ass and another on his fingers. He replaced his cock with his fingers, circling and teasing Luc's hole. One could never use too much lube. His size was definitely above average, and he didn't want to hurt his man. His lover.

*His boy.* That sounded good.

Warmth engulfed his slick fingers as he pressed two of them inside *his boy.*

Luc whimpered and grunted and whined.

*Oh yeah, that sounds even better.*

He took his time, probing and stretching. With each bump and brush of his fingers over *that spot, right...there,* in the tight channel, Luc went crazy, alternating between pleading and babbling incoherently.

*Feels so good.*

He pulled his fingers out, a little too fast if Luc's gasp gave any indication. After suiting and lubing up, he spread Luc's ass cheeks. *Beautiful.* And pushed in. A ring of tight, wet heat gripped him, forcing him to stop. "Okay?"

"Yeaaah." Luc drew in a deep breath. "Just, one second."

On Luc's exhale, the muscles gave way and let Rick in. Deeper and deeper.

"Ahhh!"

He froze, partway inside. "Luc? Babe?"

"Don't fucking stop!"

"Don't?"

"No!" Luc panted, his voice muffled by the cushion. "Keep going, and..." He flapped his hand around the back of his own neck. "You know."

*Hold him down.*

Rick grinned, before clasping the back of Luc's neck and pinning him down. "Stop being demanding." As he rocked farther into the warmth and tightness of Luc's channel, hot pleasure ran up his spine. He paused for a moment to appreciate the sight of his cock embedded halfway into Luc's beautiful asshole. "I'm in charge." A groan escaped his lips as he plunged home with a slow, steady slide. To the hilt.

"Ahh."

"Is that clear?" Pressing hard, he rolled his hips.

"Yes." Luc gasped for air. "Yes."

Tight rings of muscle gripped him. So damn tight. He waited a few seconds until Luc visibly relaxed before moving again. Ever so slowly, he pulled out until only the tip of his cock remained encased in slick warmth. But not for long. With a hard thrust, he plunged back home into his lover's warmth. Luc's strangled groan sent shock waves straight to his gut.

*Sweet heaven, nothing ever felt so good.* "You okay?"

"Yes. Yes!"

Increasing the pace, he hammered into Luc. Again and again. Holding him down, pegging his gland—owning him.

Luc yelled and panted. "Ahh! There. Harder!"

"Yes." He pistoned his hips harder, faster. Sweat ran down his temple, and his balls tightened. Tension licked at the base of his spine. He wanted Luc to come first, so he needed to hold on. As he reached around and tugged on Luc's straining, weeping cock, he growled in his ear. "C'mon, baby. C'mon. Come for me. Now."

"Ahhh!"

As Luc came, his warm sheath gripped Rick's cock, the pulsing contractions hurtling him toward completion. With a roar, he thrust. Once. Twice. And he came, shuddering and jerking as he fell over the edge into an orgasm so intense he feared losing control of his body. He slumped against Luc's back, his limbs shaking and chest heaving, giving himself a moment to catch his breath and appreciate the closeness.

Hot, sweaty skin against skin. Hearts thumping. Breaths gradually slowing and synchronizing. With a sigh, he released his hold on Luc's neck and massaged the abused muscles before sliding his hand over Luc's shoulder and arm in soothing strokes. "You okay?"

Face first into the cushion, Luc's reply was muffled. "Mm-m-mmm."

"What?"

Luc turned his head to the side. "I said you're an animal."

"What?" He reared back.

"Ah, ow. Stop, too fast."

"Sorry." He eased his cock out fully and discarded the condom.

Luc groaned and stood up. "Yep." With a smug smile, he snaked his arms around Rick's torso and all but purred as he rubbed his cheek against Rick's fur-covered chest. "An animal."

Rick chuckled and pulled Luc closer, his arms engulfing him. "I didn't hear any complaints earlier."

Luc slid his hand down Rick's back to rest on his ass. "Who said I was complaining?" He squeezed.

A growl rumbled through Rick's chest.

Luc smiled and squeezed again.

# Chapter Twenty-Six

LUC WRIGGLED AND settled into a more comfortable position on the floor. They had made themselves a cozy nest of blankets and pillows in front of the fireplace. With the warm glow of the fire on his front and the man-bear curved around his back, Luc was warm, sated, and content.

He wiggled again. Just because.

The cock nestled against his ass hardened, and Rick tightened his hold on Luc's chest. "Do that again and you'll be sorry."

Luc pushed his ass backward. "You might have to teach me a lesson." *Please!* His breath caught as Rick's answering growl rumbled through both of them, vibrating all the way down to his balls. *Holy....!*

Rick nuzzled through the hair at the back of Luc's head, the caress gentle and sweet in contrast to Rick's hot, hard cock pressing insistently against his ass crack. Luc grinned. Someone wanted in. Again. He shifted position until Rick's dick settled between his thighs, the head nudging the back of his balls. Mmm. That should get things heading in the right direction.

"We need to talk."

"Wh-what?" Definitely not the reaction he had hoped for. "What's wrong?"

Rick released his hold on Luc's chest and slid his hand downward, skimming across his stomach before settling on his hip. "Nothing, but we need to talk seriously about something."

*What the hell?* Just when he thought things couldn't be more perfect. He pulled away from Rick and turned over to face him. "Did I do something wrong?" Shit, that sounded a bit pathetic, but did he?

Rick cupped his jaw and rubbed his thumb over Luc's cheek. "No, did I?"

He frowned. Maybe postsex bliss or something had addled his brain, but what was Rick talking about? "What are you talking about?"

"Did I...? This is all kind of new, and I'm not sure I did it right."

"Huh?"

"I mean, was it good for you?"

"What?" He had a flashback of his teenage self and the awkwardness after his first fumbling hand job with another guy. He positively, seriously had no idea what was going on right now.

"Well, we haven't yet talked about this dynamic between us. I think we should probably have a safe word. I need to know if I'm getting too rough or doing something you don't like."

"Ohhh!" *Yeah. A safe word. Okay.* "Shit! For a while there..." He laughed.

Rick smiled. "What?"

"Never mind, a safe word is a good idea. Although just so you know, the idea of full-on... I mean..." His heart began to race. This was harder than he thought. What if Rick wanted more? The way Rick manhandled him and ordered him around, rough but still careful not to hurt him, was hot and satisfying, but what if Rick needed more? His gut churned and he swallowed.

"Hey!" Rick pressed a soft kiss to his lips. "Talk to me."

"I mean..." The breath he had been unconsciously holding rushed out. "I don't think I could ever be into whips and shit like that. And the thought of a ball gag strapped in my mouth makes me want to puke."

Rick laughed. "Well, thank God for that! I am definitely not into any of that either."

"Really?"

"Really. Not that there's anything wrong with that, but it's just not for me. I'm not going to lie: you make me want to take control, and I've never experienced that with anyone before."

"Never?"

Rick shook his head. "Never. You make me feel kind of...possessive, but I'm definitely not into wearing leather and wielding whips or riding crops."

Luc grinned. "Well now, let's not be too hasty. Picturing you in leather *without* the props is kind of hot."

Rick's fingers slid into his hair, and he dragged their mouths together for a hot, hard kiss that left Luc breathless and in no doubt as to who had control. *Oh, hell yeah!* "S-so, we're good then?"

"Better than. So, what about that word?"

"Oh, okay. How about 'red'?"

"No."

"Why not?"

"We need a word that cools things down."

"Huh?"

"Mmm." Rick growled. "Red ties. Red face. Red ass."

"Shit." His face burned.

"See. Red's not gonna make me stop." Rick swooped in for an intense kiss, his hot, wet lips and tongue demanding and devouring. After a few amazing minutes, their lips parted, and as their breaths and heart rates returned to normal, they both lay listening to the fire crackle and hiss.

Rick lightly stroked Luc's back, his fingers teasing the top of his ass on each downward stroke. He placed a soft kiss on Luc's forehead. "So, you'll have to choose another word."

"Yeah, okay. But I'll have to think about it."

"Sure." Rick sighed. "But one more thing."

"Mmm. What's that?"

"Am I going to lose my job for despoiling the boss's nephew?"

Luc laughed. "No, Uncle J won't care. Have you ever met him?"

"Sure, but only to discuss work."

"Believe me, he won't have a problem with you. In fact, before the whole job-swap thing, Uncle J told me he respects you. He's a pretty cool guy, and just like you, loves jazz. He throws the best black-tie parties with jazz bands and champagne and— Hey!" Luc sat up. "He's having one in two weeks at his home. You should come. You'll be my date, and I'll introduce you to him."

Rick raised an eyebrow. "You want me to attend a black-tie event at your uncle's house?"

"Well..." He grinned. "I do realize that's not really your type of scene, but there'll be jazz."

"No." Rick pulled Luc back down beside him. "Definitely not."

He trailed his fingers across Rick's chest, circling one nipple before heading toward the other. "Maybe we'll start by having a coffee with him at the office. Neutral ground. Then after a while," he completed his second circular tracing before changing direction and heading south, "if things progress..."

"Progress?"

"Between us."

"Right. What then?"

"Well, we'll work our way up to that type of family social event."

"Mmm. Still won't be my thing."

"You'd look good in a tux." One corner of his mouth curled upward as he teased the trail of hair below Rick's navel. "And I know you'll try to adapt and fit in. For me." While staring into Rick's eyes, he curled his hand around his hot, hard cock.

Rick groaned and pushed into Luc's grip. "Mmm. I suppose I could try. For you."

"And I'll do things for you too." He gave a gentle squeeze.

"Ahh!" Rick's hips jerked forward again. "Like what?"

"Like nature stuff we can do together."

"Hiking?" Rick's breaths became short and loud as Luc stroked him.

"Maybe." Without losing rhythm, Luc leaned in and whispered against Rick's mouth, "But I have another idea."

"Mmm?"

"We start out simple. You could take me outside, close to the cabin."

"And then?"

"Then, you, me, my red tie, and a tree."

"Oh, yeah. I like the sound of that." Rick grasped Luc's ass cheek in an oh-so-Master-ful way and squeezed.

Smiling, Luc bit his lip and twisted his hand on the upward stroke, eliciting a groaning growl from his lover. He couldn't wait for Rick to thrust that beautiful cock into his ass again, to fill him up like no one had before. Filling not just his body, but the hollow, empty place inside.

And he didn't know where they were headed, but he was certain that he *needed* this. He needed Rick. And their differences? Well, they could both adapt and learn to fit into each other's lives. And over time, they would work out the dynamic—

Rick swooped in and attacked his mouth, biting and devouring—in the best kind of way.

And he could learn to adapt and appreciate nature if—

Rick pinched his nipple, and a sharp little zing went straight to his cock. He groaned into Rick's mouth, barely able to think while his lumberjack fantasy man did delicious things to his body.

Luc gave another long, slow stroke to the hard flesh in his hand. And his action produced a very satisfying reaction.

It was all about give-and-take.

He smiled against Rick's mouth and then pulled back to stare at his man. *Oh, yeah.* That look in Rick's eye promised lots of give-and-take. Maybe adapting wouldn't be so difficult after all. It might even be fun.

*And so worth it.*

# Epilogue

EIGHTEEN MONTHS LATER

Luc released a shaky breath. "I'm ready."

"Okay, don't touch that blindfold, and I'll go nice and slow. We don't want any injuries."

"I trust you."

Rick's lips brushed against his temple. "I know. Thank you."

Luc clung to Rick and followed his lead, his body pressed close to his lover as the mountain breeze swirled around them, caressing bare skin and ruffling his hair.

"Okay." Rick drew in a deep breath and then released it slowly. "I can't believe how nervous I am. I really want you to like this."

"Come on; quit stalling and get on with it."

Rick chuckled. "Okay, here goes. Brace yourself."

As the blindfold fell away, Luc gasped. "Oh, my God."

Before him, on the previously level patch of dirt, stood a beautiful cabin. Constructed of cedar with a steep roof pitch and the front wall made entirely of tall panes of glass, the structure took his breath away. After months of planning, he knew the cabin would be a far cry from Rick's original plan, but it still managed to shock him with its finished beauty.

"It's... It's..."

"Ours."

"Yeah." In awe, he gazed at Rick's labor of love.

"Do you like it?"

"Yep. You did good."

"We did good." Rick hugged him closer. "We make a good team. It's amazing how well our ideas blended, and pooling our resources made it possible. I especially like your contribution of indoor plumbing."

"Yeah." A short chuckle escaped as he thought of the battle of wills between them over that issue. "It was money well spent. I'm glad we found a way to make it work."

Rick stared into his eyes for a long intense moment. "Yeah, me too."

With a smile, Luc burrowed into the warmth of his lumberjack man's arms and chest. Exactly where he belonged. They'd had their struggles over the past year, learning to compromise and pushing each other out of their comfort zones. It turned out that Rick looked spectacular in a tux. And Luc had come around to the joys of nature. Sort of. Okay, he was working on it.

Rick gave him a squeeze. "Let's go inside."

"Okay."

"Wait! There's a proper way to cross the threshold."

"Wh-what the hell?" His unmanly squawk sent hidden critters scuttling, and the world tipped as Rick slung him over his shoulder as if he weighed nothing and carried him toward their new home.

The blood rushed to Luc's head, among other places, and he mumbled a few choice phrases. This was not the second or even third time Rick had done this. It was becoming a habit.

"Fucking caveman."

"You love it."

He scoffed, but yeah, he really did. "Am I going to get the grand tour?"

"That's the plan."

"Can I at least be upright when I see the inside?"

"Mmm. No."

"What? Ahhh!" He released an undignified squawk as Rick did that...thing as he shifted his hold, high on Luc's thigh. "Hey, watch the handsy stuff."

"You love it."

*Yeah, I really do.*

Rick carried him up the stairs and into the cabin. From the upside-down perspective, Luc surveyed the space. Polished wooden floors, warm colors, stone fireplace, and surprisingly spacious. "Come on." He gave Rick's ass cheeks a few slaps. "Let me up, you big Neanderthal."

The room spun as Rick maneuvered him from over his shoulder and laid him on the thick, soft rug on the floor. High ceilings, wooden beams, a brass ceiling fan. *Nice.* Shifting his legs, he allowed Rick to settle into the familiar position, cradled between his thighs.

Rick braced himself on his elbows above him. "So, this is it. Do you like it?"

Luc chuckled and wrapped his arms around Rick's neck. "I can't see much from down here."

"I figured we'd inspect each room from the ground up."

"You're an idiot."

"Watch it."

Luc bit his lip and smiled. "Sorry, Sir."

Rick hummed and then swooped in for a very thorough kiss, sending Luc's senses spinning and his mind blank. Too soon, Rick pulled his mouth away. "Do you like it?"

Dazed, Luc stared at the lush lips hovering over him. "Ohh, yeeaah."

"I meant, the cabin—this living room."

"Well..." He slid his fingers over Rick's close-cropped beard. "From what I'm looking at..." He locked in eye contact. "It's everything I'd ever hoped for and exactly what I need." He smoothed his hand over Rick's hair. "Exactly. What about you? Are you happy?"

Rick's gaze roved over Luc's face. "It's not what I'd originally planned, but it's..." He stroked Luc's cheek with his forefinger.

"It's what?"

Rick smiled. "Better. Different to what I thought I needed, but better."

Luc smiled so hard his face ached. "Yeah?"

"And I..." Rick's smile disappeared, and he pressed his lips oh-so-gently to Luc's in a soft, lingering kiss. "I think... I know..." He stared, his focus never wavering from Luc's eyes. "I love...*it*."

Luc's heart thumped in a crazy rhythm as he let the words sink in. When it came to emotional moments, his lover was still a man of few words. But a few, three to be exact, was all he needed.

Beard bristles tickled his palms as he cupped Rick's face. "'It'? Well, I have to tell you that I love 'it' too." He grinned with a sure-to-be-dopey smile, but he didn't care.

Rick leaned down and bit Luc's earlobe, before growling another three words into his ear. "Pants off. Now."

His breath hitched.

*Oh, yes, Sir.*

# About the Author

CM Corett is lucky enough to have two careers she loves—cartography and writing. She has lived in the USA and traveled the world gathering inspiration for her stories, but the beautiful beaches of Western Australia will always be her home. She is an avid reader and writer of love between men, and also loves movies, superheroes, and video games with awesome graphics. She hates housework and anyone who expects her to notice (or care about) the dust on top of the fridge. CM does not limit herself to one sub-genre. She writes contemporary, historical, sci-fi, and time travel...and she may have a few paranormal ideas awaiting her attention.

Website: www.cmcorett.com

Facebook: www.facebook.com/CMCorett

Twitter: @cmcorettauthor

# Other books by this author

*2 Days Later*

# Also Available from NineStar Press

# Connect with NineStar Press

www.ninestarpress.com

www.facebook.com/ninestarpress

www.facebook.com/groups/NineStarNiche

www.twitter.com/ninestarpress

www.tumblr.com/blog/ninestarpress

www.ingramcontent.com/pod-product-compliance
Lightning Source LLC
Chambersburg PA
CBHW060604190726
48283CB00003B/1147